John Lancaster Spalding

Thoughts and theories of life and education

John Lancaster Spalding

Thoughts and theories of life and education

ISBN/EAN: 9783337215347

Printed in Europe, USA, Canada, Australia, Japan

Cover: Foto ©Andreas Hilbeck / pixelio.de

More available books at **www.hansebooks.com**

THOUGHTS AND THEORIES

OF

LIFE AND EDUCATION

BY

J. L. SPALDING

Bishop of Peoria

Hope like a star gleams in the breast
Of him who labors without rest,
In Truth's sweet service and in Love's

CHICAGO

A. C. McCLURG AND COMPANY

1899

CONTENTS.

THOUGHTS AND THEORIES

OF

LIFE AND EDUCATION.

———•———

CHAPTER I.

THOUGHTS AND THEORIES.

When the rose is fair it makes the garden fair,
When the soul is fair its beauty all may share.

IN the course of ages there have been a few
in whose company it is possible to think
high thoughts in a noble spirit; but there has
been and is but one with whom it is possible to
lead the life of the soul and feel that it is like
the life of God, — he is the Master, Christ Jesus,
who alone makes us understand and realize that
God is our Father, and that our business on
earth is to grow into the divine image by right
loving and doing. To know God is to transcend
the contradictions and dark mysteries of human
existence, and to taste the pure joy and peace
which children feel when their father is near.

So long as thou canst believe, with all thy heart, in thy heavenly Father, nothing can trouble thy deepest soul; for, since He is, nothing is hard to bear, and all will be well. As there is no stable equilibrium in the life of an individual, there is none in that of a community, a state, or a church. The inexorable command is, — Go forward or fall back, grow or decay. Thy life is possible only through communion with God, with nature, and with thy fellowman; and thou canst educate thyself only by holding thy mind and heart in conscious and sympathetic contact with God, with nature, and with thy fellowmen. Separation is mutilation, isolation is death. To attempt to gain knowledge without the faith and feeling that God lives within His universe, that nature is His vesture and thou thyself a member of the whole human organism, is to take the path which leads to hopeless doubt, to intellectual despair. After however much labor and pain, thou shalt at last be forced to cry out with the poet, that it breaks thy heart to know that man can know nothing. But if, with yearning thought and tireless effort, thou reachest forth to all that is divine, and natural, and nobly human, thou shalt surely gain new access of life, new strength of mind and heart, and little by little come to feel that the arms of the Eternal are twined lovingly about thee. The Divine

Power is manifest in what lives, grows, and ful-
fils itself, rather than in what is finished and
complete.

We cannot comprehend what awakens the
purest and profoundest emotions. They who
feel God's presence inquire not into the nature
of His being, as a child reposing on a mother's
breast asks not how or why she is fair. " It is
not always necessary," says Goethe, " that truth
take definite shape; it may be enough that it
hover about us like a spirit and produce harmony." God is before all, within all, above all,
— eternal, immanent, transcendent.

The deeper and purer one's religion, the
higher and richer his moral life; and as moral
worth increases, faith in God is confirmed.
Truth and love are the best, though all men
should fall away from them; and faith in the
love of God is the life of the soul, however few
there be who drink from this fountain head.
Believe, then, and love; and so live that they
who come near to thee may feel the divine
influence.

When we think of the vast bulk of the earth;
of the unimaginable force with which it turns
on its axis; of the velocity with which it circles
around the sun, fully one-and-a-half million
miles a day, — and then add to this the forces
of the innumerable heavenly bodies, as they

revolve in swiftest motion, the power of God
from which all this springs so overwhelms us
that we seem to cease to be. As man's strength
vanishes into nothingness in the presence of the
Divine Power, so in the presence of the Divine
Wisdom, Goodness, and Love, his knowledge,
goodness, and love become as though they were
not. Thou alone art, O my God! and I but
exist; do with me as Thou wilt; it is enough
for me to have been conscious, for a moment
even, of Thy almighty power and goodness.

> " If in us dwelt not God's own might
> How could the godlike give delight ? "

We live in God ; and since He lives eternally,
why shall not we also who are partakers of His
life? It is with life as with evil, — the mystery
lies in its being at all, not ·in its never ending.
As in the presence of some great calamity,
which destroys cities and lays waste whole
provinces, we bow to the inscrutable will of God,
feeling that explanation is hopeless, so let us
behave in all the happenings of life, in the small
as in the great. He hides in dark clouds of
mystery, and his ways are unsearchable ; but He
watches over us, and what He does is rightly
done. We seek only what we have in a way
already found, at the least, as a longing and
aspiration ; and if we seek God, it is because we

feel within the inmost heart the need of Him to save us from falling into nothingness. He Himself is in our yearning for Him and in our seeking; and therefore when we ask, we receive; when we seek, we find; when we strive to know Him, He is near; when we love Him, He is ours. They whose souls this truth has penetrated are not disturbed by doubts and difficulties. They have found their Father and are at peace. Live with thy soul, and find God there, and thou shalt not need to pray for miracles.

All things fulfil the law of their being, — the flowers bloom and scatter fragrance, the tree bears its fruit, the stars keep their appointed places. Let thy will hold thee too, steadfast and true. What lesser creatures will-less do, do thou willingly. What is far is also near. Ninety million miles away, the sun is still close to us and keeps us alive. So God, who seems infinitely remote, is within our inmost being, impelling us to thought and love. We know only as we are affected; and our thoughts of God and the Universe are but the expression of their influence on us. That which is not within us is for us as though it were not. To those alone who feel God's presence in the soul as the supreme reality, do nature and history proclaim His infinite power and goodness. We never comprehend what we adore; for to comprehend is to dominate, and we cannot adore that which is subject to us. Hence, God and all the deep realities of life are mysteries which we feel and accept, but cannot understand. Hence, too, we never lay hold of the truths of religion with the firmness and definiteness with which we grasp the truths of science. We know them only so far as we feel them; and, therefore, right disposition and right life are essential to the maintenance of wholesome and vigorous faith. Strive ceaselessly to increase thy power of admiration, enthusiasm, reverence, and awe; for God is with thee and is in all thou beholdest and knowest; and if thou be great enough and pure enough, thou shalt feel His presence, and rejoice in Him and His work. He is not an abstraction, but the infinite reality; and the process of abstraction leads from, not to Him. He cannot be deduced from phrases or confined in formulas. If thou wouldst know Him, feel after Him with thy whole being, — yearning, hoping, believing, loving, and doing; and He shall become as real for thee as thy very self. The love of God is the only love which is not a chain. Make Thou me, O God! Mould and fashion me as Thou knowest and willest, and not as I think and desire.

> Virtue is beauty; in a noble mind
> Whatever is most fair thou 'lt surely find.

Without God, thou canst do nothing; but in thy struggle for wisdom and virtue, look to thyself; for, if thou do thy part, His help will not be lacking. If religion is true, the religious gain all; if it is false, they lose nothing; for their joys, even here, are higher and purer than anything worldlings know. Let there be light within thy mind, and thy life shall become a light-irradiating centre for others. We cannot honor God by making man appear worse than he is, since to serve Him rightly we must make ourselves and others better. We feel our dependence, not on nature, for we are conscious of our superiority to matter, but on the Infinite Spirit; and thus self-consciousness is a confession of God's existence. With me there dwells one greater than I. Whether I think or hope, I am conscious of His presence. He is behind all I see or hear or touch. It is He who makes me know that I live; it is He who makes me feel that death is apparent only. The creation is not finished. My Father, says the Divine Master, works even until now. Since God is still busy with His task, how shall we be idle? Or is it not a godlike thing to work with the Almighty? The light dawns from within the mind and heart. What has not been seen and felt there, will not body itself forth in right words or deeds. No one can do more than

show thee the way to the highest. Thou must
thyself walk therein, if thou wouldst reach the
end. Thy misery is within thyself. Become other
and higher, and life will be good enough for
thee. However great the darkness in thy mind,
the world is still full of light, and God is over
all. Be not discouraged by thy past, but know
that, whatever it has been, the best may still be
thine. Seek truth for thyself; for if thou think-
est of others, thou art not thinking of truth.
The power to know more and more, without end,
gives us kinship with the Eternal Wisdom. It
is God who fills us with the craving to know yet
more what we know, and to love yet more what
we love. A pure heart is better than a strong
mind; and honesty, whether or not the best
policy, is better than all policy. Think not that
God exists to make thee happy. He exists for
Himself, and thou canst find happiness only in
giving thyself wholly to Him. Thou canst not
improve others, unless thou continue to improve
thyself. If thy words are to have efficacy, thy
life must give it to them. Thy proper business
is to make thyself worthy; but thou canst do
this only by holding thyself in communion with
God, and in helpful harmony with the best interests of those with whom thou livest. In this
way alone canst thou find peace and contentment; for if thou live not with God and for thy

fellowmen, thy life shall grow to be barren and burdensome to thee. Though thou thyself fail, rejoice that it has been given to another to do nobly; for if thou art capable of envy, thou art incapable of wisdom. Since truth is the highest, being the centre of goodness and love, truthfulness is the best. If God has made thee capable of doing any real thing, thou must do it, or in all eternity it will not be done. The highest is for thee, since God wills to give Himself to thee. Thy whole business is to make thyself worthy. Under all our knowledge of things lie the ideas of force, substance, space, and time, which are beyond our comprehension. In the same way above, behind, within the world, as it appears to us, there is an infinite reality, a power which makes the world what it is, and which we cannot comprehend, but which we call truth, goodness, beauty, absolute life, God, — feeling certain that the more nobly we think of this essential Being, the more nearly we approach His unfathomable nature. The scientific process is not so much a rising from facts to principles, as it is a transformation of the world of the senses into a world of forces and laws. Thought-powers — for such are force and law — lie at the heart of the universal fact. In the more practical phases of science also, that which most attracts us is not the having and holding and sensual enjoyment

of things, but the dominion over them, — the
ability to turn them to increase the power and
quality of our life.   The centre of gravity of all
thinking and striving lies not in what the world
is or may be made, but in what man is and may
become.   A single human soul outweighs the
whole material universe; for matter has meaning
and value only for souls.   When the inner life
becomes a world for itself, it cannot be shaken
by what comes from without.   Truth lies not
abroad, but in the deeps; and when the soul is
driven back upon itself by the flaming walls of
space, it finds its true home, where even that
which in the external world it recognizes as
apparent only, becomes real as part of its experience.   We live, indeed, in time and place; but
the more profound our soul-life becomes, the
better do we understand that it cannot be confined in space or supported by ideas that are
not eternal Truth, — Truth which we can never
fully possess; but which is the motive and end
of all our striving.   The stream of life flows not
from the present to the future, but from the
present to eternity.   The future shall never be
ours, — shall never be, at all, as the future; but
we may, if we will, live always with what is
eternal, with truth and love, — with God.   He
who lives rightly in the present, lives for and in
eternity, which is the proper home of the spirit,

whose life is at once in the past, the present, and the future. In the midst of transitory and apparent things, it is conscious of a world which is real and permanent. Rising above the lapses of time, it sees the nothingness of all that passes away.

The minute thou hast lost or misused, eternity shall not make good for thee. The primary duty is not to make life pleasant and beautiful, but to make it true and good, by holding it in communion with the Infinite Spirit from whom it springs. If it be true and good, it will be also pleasant and beautiful. Learn to live in the divine world, and thy life will become divine. Self-improvement is, at bottom, moral improvement, development of character; for it is this that makes a man, and without this intellectual and æsthetic culture is a futile thing. It requires time and pains to learn to do what it is most profitable to do. If, therefore, thou wouldst do well any useful thing, spare not labor, nor think a lifetime long. Our action is feeble and ineffectual unless it spring from our innermost being, from the thought and love which make us what we are. Become a living soul and utter thyself, and thy words and deeds shall kindle life in others. Hold thyself aloof from those who think in herds, who estimate all things at the value the crowd puts upon them.

To think is to make an inner conquest of the objects of thought. What we know we have overcome. Knowledge, like love, triumphs over all things. Bring forth within thyself higher truth and love, ànd thou shalt find thyself a new being in a new world.

> From within, from within, springs life's deep source
> And backward to its fountain circles its course.

Thy whole strength is in God; in Him all thy power of faith, hope, and love. From Him and to Him all thy thinking and striving move. Without Him thou wert nothing; and with Him all divine things are possible for thee.

It is a mistake to assume that it is harder to know the whole than the parts, the invisible than the visible, the eternal than the temporal. We know ourselves and God as wholes; and this is the most immediate knowledge. When we strive to grasp matter, it melts into the invisible, becomes atoms and ether, — a system of forces. Eternity is plain; time and space are the puzzle. It is the radical vice of our present philosophy and education that they teach young souls to doubt that of which they are most certain, — thus banishing them from their true home, and leaving them helpless and hopeless in a God-forsaken universe. When we affirm that duty is the supreme law of life, that all ideals are subject to moral ideals, we doubtless utter a great truth; but duty, even when it is reverenced, is associated with stern and chilling thoughts; it does not raise and cheer us like the voice of love. The mother watching by the side of her sick child would shrink from the thought that she is doing what duty bids: duty is swallowed in love. The Saviour spoke not of duty, but of love; and millions of hearts respond to his appeal for hundreds who are swayed by the cold and imperative command of duty. Duty is morality, love is religion, transforming morality into righteousness, which is life. Loving is the only true living. God sees all things and is not disturbed. Canst thou not retain composure, and work in thy little world with a calm spirit, however much the storms buffet thee and men fret and complain? It is but for a moment. Unimaginable lengths of time precede each man's birth and follow his death. Between these two immensities the longest life shrivels to the point of vanishment.

He who in youth labors to improve himself in knowledge and virtue is cheered and upborne by a high and joyful spirit; and in old age he will look back on a life rich in good deeds and in happy memories.

> ' T is sweet to think of labors past
> When now the haven 's gained at last.

Fix thy thought and desire solely upon the best; then if fame and wealth become thine also, thou shalt know how to enjoy them in innocence and purity. So think and act as to be what thou wouldst have men consider thee. What the youth most yearns for is the surest indication of what the man shall attain. Be thy own best friend, which thou canst be, if thou art a steadfast friend to truth and virtue. Look upon life as a succession of opportunities for improving thyself and for doing good; so shall its every moment, whether of pleasure or of pain, of success or of failure, bring thee profit; and little by little thou shalt come to know many things and to love much. Thou shalt learn to suffer with fortitude and to enjoy with moderation, to be helpful to thy friends and just to thy foes. Thy sympathies shall widen, thy thoughts grow nearer truth; and thy gratitude to God, the giver of all good, become as much a part of thyself, as the breath which feeds the flame of thy life.

Turn resolutely from whatever weakens or discourages. The best strength is strength of mind; the best wealth, a loving heart. Whoever may have wronged thee, wrong not thyself by complaining. If thou art a lover of virtue rather than of thyself, thou shalt not be tempted to envy the superiority of others. To be without evil thoughts, says Æschylus, is God's best gift. Think not of profit, whether to thy name or thy purse; but live in thy work, glad and thankful that thou art able to do and love it. Better not be spoken of at all than to be praised with lies.

The microscope makes marvellous revelations; but if things appeared so to the naked eye, the world would be a place of horrors. So Science teaches profitable truth; but if the mind were fitted to a purely mechanical scheme of things, life would be unbearable. It is not difficult to know truth, if by constant exercise we keep the mind open and the heart pure, as athletes perform their feats with ease when they keep themselves in proper training. To be rich in love, in wisdom, in knowledge, in well doing, in friends to whom we have brought joy and strength, is to be rich indeed. What hot disputes, mingled with anathemas, once raged about the existence of the antipodes; but when the fact of their existence was made palpable, to accept it was no longer a sin against orthodoxy. Let us seek truth in the spirit of mildness and humility, and learn to possess our souls in peace. We imagine that we need not give heed to the commonplaces; but the best wisdom lies in them, and a real mind will strive to rethink them and to clothe them anew, thus giving them fresh meaning.

That which distinguishes great minds from
the common is not so much a difference in ideas
as a difference in the way they are held.   Ideas
take possession of great minds and transform
themselves into their substance; while in ordinary minds their presence is casual and transitory.   In men of genius we rarely meet with
anything original; but we find in them truths
with which we are more or less acquainted,
grasped with fresh power and set forth with new
meaning and beauty.   The Kingdom of God is
within.   Renounce thyself; love, and be meek
and humble of heart, and thou shalt find it, —
this is the method and secret of Jesus.   Cultivate the power of going out of thyself that thou
mayst be able to see and appreciate what is
good and fair in others.   Thus shalt thou acquire an open mind and a large heart, which
are better than all the gifts of fortune; "for a
man's life consisteth not in the abundance of the
things he possesseth."

As infirm health or defects of body, by
barring the way to the common pursuits, have
impelled some to cultivate their spiritual endowments, and thus have been for them the
occasions of worth and distinction; so is there
hardly any misfortune or disadvantage which
the wise will not convert to opportunities of
larger and truer life.   The reality within and

around us is more beautiful and more wonderful than all that the fairy tales tell of, than the
enchanted regions of which poets have sung;
but its divine perfections are hidden from us,
because we are heedless, dull, and unawakened,
and like mere animals move about in worlds
unrealized. It is the business and purpose of
religion, as it is of culture, to rouse and thrill
us with the consciousness that God and all the
divine things to which we aspire, are with us,
even here, if we would but look and hearken.
Therefore the lovers of perfection are busy
striving to teach us that the Kingdom of God
is within; and that to hope to win joy and
peace by getting money, and surrounding ourselves with the things money buys, is a delusion,
— is as though we should expect to find home
in foreign lands and those we love among
strangers; as though we should imagine that
possessions are more precious than life, which
alone gives them value.

To be one of a crowd, in brilliant parlors,
where men and women wear fine clothes and say
silly nothings; to sit at tables laden with rich
meats and wines, for which one has no appetite;
to ride in showy equipages merely to see and
be seen; to breathe the foul air of theatres, to
look at the poor acting of poor plays, or at
vulgar exhibitions of the human body; to travel

because one is tired of home; to buy books
which one does not read, and pictures for which
one does not care; to make great display in
which there is little enjoyment; to seek company to escape the dreariness and monotony of
one's own thoughts, — this is the life of the idle
rich, this the boon which money brings. The
case of those who are intent on getting money
is hardly better than that of those who are busy
spending it. They waste their powers in accu-
mulating what they cannot enjoy; and, while
they heap up gold, their minds are starved, their
hearts are withered, and their consciences made
callous. They become the victims of their success, and die great capitalists, but stunted men.
To be thought indifferent to what is called
civilization is a matter of small moment for one
who knows that the good of life lies in the right
disposition of mind and heart, and not in the
things a man possesses, which, if they are desired
and sought after as though they were paramount,
are a hindrance.

The two laws of which St. Paul speaks —
the law of the mind and the law of the members
— is what is meant by the higher and the
lower self. Wisdom and peace are found by
those who succeed in bringing the inferior and
intermittent self into subjection to the higher
and permanent self. In other words, the re-

ward of righteousness is life, and the wages of sin is death. The right disposition — purity of intention, simplicity of aim, modesty, teachable-ness, and the desire to do right — helps us to insight into the highest and holiest truth better than much learning. It is this which sometimes makes plain to the lowly-minded what is hidden from great philosophers. If we could but sweeten our temper, overcome our hardness and pride, and annul our sensuality — whatever else is needful would easily be found. They who bring us peace and joy, who calm and invigor-ate our minds, are not merely spiritual benefac-tors; they impart a sense of physical comfort, and help us to triumph over bodily infirmities.

Happiness is a poor word to express our deepest need. The child is happy when it has cakes and toys; the maid when she can marry her sad lover; the mother when her baby is fat and fair; the laborer when his wages are high; the farmer when his crops are good; the miser when his pile of gold is growing; — but all this is hardly better than the happiness of animals in the midst of rich and abundant pasture; and if we take the word in this sense, we may say that only the unhappy know and yearn for the best, — for that which makes us human and akin to God. If I lived in a great city, or in a palace, or wore costly habiliments, or drank delicious

wines, I should not love more or know more or
be more; and since the hope of purer love,
truer knowledge, and diviner power of life, is
what refreshes and upholds me in all my longing and striving,— why should I desire and seek
the things which certainly cannot strengthen, but
may weaken and destroy this hope?

As they who do not speak the same language
cannot understand one another, so neither can
they whose thoughts and aims make them inhabit-
ants of different worlds.   In vain they agree to
use the same words, to accept the same formulas ; so long as their world is not the same, no
real union of mind and heart is possible.

> Truth and love rejoice together,
> But each is sad without the other.

They do not know and love who feel that they
know and love enough ; and they are not grate-
ful who believe they have done enough. Be
not led astray by the desires, ambitions, and
thoughts which are prevalent among those who
hope to find peace and joy in high place, or in
much wealth, or in a multitude of friends, or in
sensual indulgence; for they are not to be
found in these things, but are the blessings of
those whose hearts are pure and loving, and
whose minds are luminous with truth.

Tranquillity of mind, which if not happiness

is inseparable from it, belongs only to those who follow the example and the teaching of the Saviour,— to the lowly minded, the pure hearted, the peace loving, the truth seeking, and the God trusting. Neither poverty nor wealth, neither obscurity nor fame, neither dulness nor genius, neither love nor its absence, neither knowledge nor ignorance, can secure this inner blessedness for which all yearn, and which only they who become as little children find. The worst enemies of religion are the formalists, they who ban and bar for a phrase or a ceremony, but are careless of truth and love. They are the children of the Scribes and Pharisees whom Christ denounced and who crucified him. Thy private opinion, if honestly and seriously formed, has for thee more vital worth than the public opinion of thy country or of many countries. A little is enough. A single dish is all that is needful, the Saviour said to Martha, busy with preparing a feast: and when we have learned to be content with little, fair Freedom comes with a smile to welcome us to the inner world where Truth leads Liberty by the hand, and the soul tastes delights which the senses can never give.

The lover of truth, like a fresh-hearted boy, looks to each new day as to a new life, in which he shall find he knows not what of joy and

beauty. Like lovers and friends who watch
for the coming of those they love, he is alert to
catch the faintest stirrings of the winged messengers who draw near to bring him high and
holy thoughts; and if but a single celestial
visitant make glad the day, his mind is filled
with light and his heart with thankfulness; and
so for him every day is God's day, given him
that he may learn to know and love.

Once we have learned the secret of labor,
which never wearies and never loses heart, all
the mysteries of the success of heroes and
saints, of philosophers and poets, are made
plain to us. Nothing but ceaseless effort is
difficult, and nothing else achieves aught of
permanent value. Only the habitually thought-
ful are prepared to take advantage of the mo-
ments of inspiration which come to all, but
which for the most depart unnoticed and un-
used. It is the welcome given to these heavenly
messengers by saints and by poets that makes
them a race apart. The truth which with in-
audible flutterings and magnetic thrills circles
near me to-day, like a humming-bird among
the flowers, may, if unheeded, take flight and
nevermore return. For me it emerges for
briefest space, from the bosom of the eternal;
but, if I care not for it, it seeks again its everlasting home.

When I was younger I longed to meet with great minds that I might learn from them the secret of the mysteries which haunt the soul; but at last I came to understand that nothing but patient watching and solitary study can lead us where divine worlds break upon the view. The lower our sympathy descends, the more human are we, and the more godlike; for God's mercy is over all His works. What do we know diviner than the love of mothers and of all true lovers, which stoops to the humblest service with a sense of joy and exaltation? They who mount to whatever heights must still dwell in spirit in the lowly vales where life begins, on penalty of losing the best and holiest which life can give.

Amid endless variety of circumstance, — in cities and in deserts, in palaces and in huts, on sea and on land, in arctic and in tropic regions — men live and relish life. They adapt themselves to all situations, and are brave and hearty everywhere, if only there is inner health and harmony. He who breathes the air of the intellect and swims in a current of ideas, is rich enough, though poor. The wide earth is his home, and whatever he knows and cherishes is his property. God who sees the universe sees that all is well, and if we were great enough, life would be good enough; but we sojourn in the senses, and the real world is hidden from us though it is close to every mind. Be not overawed or discouraged by the noise made about popular names; nor by the pomp with which men of wealth and official eminence are surrounded. These things are a hindrance to right life, to growth of mind, to integrity of character, to elevation of thought and purity of soul; and those who are perked in a glittering show seldom have any other distinction than that which is conferred by circumstances; whereas thou, hidden from the world, art left free to live within, with God and with all that the noblest and greatest of thy race have thought and loved. The impulse to utter what is deepest in us is irresistible; but when he who builds or writes or speaks or sings or paints, thinks of the praise or the money his work shall bring, he acts in the spirit of a hireling, and the divine mood dies within him. The cause of all our shallowness and insincerity is that our ear is turned to catch the rumor of the world, or the approval of one or several, and is not lowered to the still whisperings of the soul. We cannot know what worth there is in our words and deeds, nor is it important that we should know. It is our business to think and to do with whatever power God has given us; and while we so act, our life is good and healthful. Of well doing as of health we are but feebly conscious; for, by right action, self is merged in the infinite world of truth and goodness. We do not know the worth of our words and deeds, nor can we know whether we have yet thought and done the best possible for us; and it is, therefore, the part of wisdom to continue striving for higher knowledge and virtue, even to the verge of the grave, that we may not only live, but that we die, still hoping and learning. Fear is our great enemy, — fear of the world, of wicked men and wicked tongues; fear of unpopularity, of loss in business or in social standing; fear of the disapproval of the ignorant and prejudiced, of liars and fools; fear of friends and servants; of wives and children; and so we walk trembling, as though we picked our way amid jungles where venomous reptiles and beasts of prey haunt. We have no heart, no courage to be ourselves; to think our thoughts and live our lives, with a noble scorn of whoever would lessen our liberty, or bid us halt in the way which God has opened for us.

The life of dissipation, that of gamblers, drunkards, and libertines, kills the soul; the life of business, that of merchants, manufacturers, and money-lenders, stifles it; the life of toil, that of laborers and drudges, holds it in the prison of semi-consciousness; the life of society, that of

the idle rich, gives it but leave to show itself like
a pet or a clown; the life of the family, that of
husbands, wives, and children, clips its wings
and reduces it to the condition of a barn-yard
fowl.   Only in communion with God, with
nature, and with great minds, yet here or passed
beyond, can the soul prosper and know the infinite worth of its divine being.   When everywhere there is pretension and mere seeming, be
thankful that thou art permitted to stand aside
from the clamorous and blind rushings of the
crowd, to dwell with thy own soul, in the presence of what is eternally true and good, that so
thou mayst become a real and not an apparent
man.   Let that prevail which brings the highest
good to men, which bears them nearer to infinite
truth and love; and if thy private interests and
prejudices stand a hair's breadth in the way, let
them be shattered as by the breath of God.

We here in America are the most prodigious
example of success which history records.   In
little more than a century we have subdued a
continent to the uses of civilized man; we have
built cities, railways, and telegraphs; we have
invented all kinds of machines to do all kinds of
work; we have established a school and a newspaper in every hamlet; our wealth is incalculable;
our population is counted by tens of millions;
and yet in spite of all we are a disappointment

to ourselves and to the world, because we have failed in the supreme end of human effort, — the making man himself a wiser, nobler, diviner being. We have uttered no thoughts which have illumined the nations; we have not felt the thrill of immortal loves; we are not buoyed by a faith and hope which are as firm rooted as the rock-ribbed mountains. We have had no prophet, no poet, no philosopher, no saint, no supreme man in any art or science. We have trusted to matter as the most real thing; we have lived on the surface, amid shows, and our souls have not drunk of the deep infinite source of life. Our religion and our education are cherished for the practical ends which they serve; for the support they give to our political institutions, while these institutions themselves are made a kind of fetish. The people have become less disinterested, less high-minded, less really intelligent; and among their leaders it is rare to find one who is distinguished either by strength and cultivation of mind or by purity and integrity of character. Are we destined to become the most prodigious example of failure as of success, recorded by history?

Politics and practical life have indispensable uses, but they are not everything; and those who speak to the soul, who thrill it with nobler thoughts, with higher views of truth and visions

3

of a more celestial beauty, do also necessary
work, for without it man would be little more
than a shrewder kind of animal; and in the
world by which we are surrounded, the spiritual
sense, the sense for things which have no material uses, needs cultivation far more than the
faculty for contriving and getting. Our education is, as Emerson says, a system of despair.
It is a device to help us to gain a livelihood, to
prepare the young to become clerks or merchants or mechanics or lawyers or preachers, —
a key which unlocks the world of story-books
and newspapers; but in education as a divine
force, whereby a nobler race may be formed, we
have no faith. We have confidence that our
machinery shall be made more and more perfect, but no hope that it shall be put in the
hands of more godlike men and women. We
are influenced by climate, by the quality of the
soil we till, by the implements we use, by the
kind of work we do, and by whatever encom-
passes us; but a good climate will not of itself
make good men, nor will good machines. The
dwellers in our fine houses are ordinary people,
and show no tendency to become equal to the
splendor of their habitations. The travellers in
our luxurious cars and steamships have vulgar
thoughts and aims, and long not for anything
higher.

It seems doubtful whether the environment which civilization has created tends to improve men, however superior the civilized man be to the savage. He reaches a certain point, and then his wealth and machinery become hindrances to further progress. Shall we never see such men and women as the knights and fair ladies with whom the rich imagination of youth peoples the castles of the centuries that are gone? The kind of man the young so easily imagine and steadfastly believe in must be possible. Shall we not yet redeem the promise which gleams in the stars, laughs in the flowers, leaps in the heart of childhood, and is current with the thoughts and loves of poets and virgins? We crave for wealth and sensual delights, because we have not made ourselves capable of knowledge and love.

The truthseeker in his narrow room is happy enough; the youth and maid find a paradise simply in loving each other. They who mock the scholar and the lover are but barbarians who think the good of life is found in display or in the gratification of appetite. The bliss of poets, the rapture of saints, the tranquil mind of the wise, the sweet heart of virgins and mothers, are beyond their imagining. They own not the stars and the clouds, but only the things they touch or taste or wear or flaunt before the envious eyes of the vulgar.   How shall they understand that only what we know and love and can do, is ours; that genuine titles of ownership are written on the mind and heart, and not on parchment and paper?

The misfortunes which throw us back upon ourselves, upon the inner source of life, thereby driving us nearer to God, are blessings, however unwelcome or rudely given.   The friend who has forsaken me was a distraction, the money which I have lost a hindrance.   The disagreeable surroundings in which I find myself compel me to live in a higher sphere, as lack of recognition from the world reminds me that approval is wisely sought only in one's own mind and conscience.

Make thy heart pure and listen to the voice within, and thou shalt not need to ask for proof of God's existence.   He is with thee, and the theories and disputations of the learned cannot banish Him.   The earth is not an immovable centre, as was believed of old; and yet the sun and the stars keep their places and nothing is changed, and so God abides, however the thoughts of men widen and diverge.   He is with thee, the God of thy fathers, thy own Father; not an All-nothing, not a stream without whence or whither, rising and ending nowhere; but the Infinite Power who makes thee, who makes thee capable of

faith and hope, of truth and love, and saves thee
from the abyss of despair and death. To live
habitually in the company of great thoughts and
under the impulse of generous emotions is as
near the blessed life as one may hope to
approach on earth, while petty thoughts and
selfish desires attend the weak and miserable.
They drive them to envy, hate, and sensuality;
for, so long as they are possessed by such
thoughts and desires, they are displeasing to
themselves, and seek self-forgetfulness in dwell-
ing on the sins and misfortunes of others, or in
yielding to their animal nature, or they dwindle
and harden until they become mere getters or
hoarders of money. That we may escape such
a fate let us refresh ourselves day by day with
rethinking some vital truth, with reviving some
noble sentiment, that these heavenly powers may
guard us at our work and keep us worthily active
and beneficent. If we have not the ability to do
this unassisted, let us have recourse to a genuine
book, choosing what will suit our purpose from
the Gospels or the Imitation, or from the life of a
saint or a sage, or from the pages of an inspired
poet. No formality is necessary and little time
is required; and if we persevere we shall find
ourselves rising to higher and serener worlds,
where pettiness and baseness fall away, and
God's presence is revealed. Merely to know

that God is, fills me with such joy and confidence that the ills of life seem vain and transitory.

The conviction that all which I most desire and admire has its source in the Eternal, who makes truth and love the most real things, gives me such contentment, that my ignorance and doubts, my weakness and faults, cease to disturb my peace of soul. Whatever confusion may arise in the world around me, whatever direction the course of events may take, I rest in the thought that, above and within all, there is a living Power who guides the whole to ends diviner than I can conceive. This is enough; I throw all my little weight of care on Him; a sense of security takes possession of me, and I am as unafraid as a child rocked by a mother's hand. I look away from sorrow and death, and all the agonies of bruised hearts and despairing souls, to where, behind the veil of sense, God lives and loves forever; and I feel that with Him are things unknown to mortal minds, full of divine meaning and benevolence, into which the miseries of man enter, and are transformed into peace and joy, falling into the tranquil bosom of the Eternal, like tears of repentant children on the white and tender breasts of mothers. When I see flowers bending their fair heads in the pleasant air, they seem to me to be souls, who in adoring God blossom into beauty and fragrance. We live on the fat earth which breaks into myriad forms of life, and we feel that it is good to be here. We call it our mother, our country, our home; but it hardly occurs to us that, if the sun's heat were withdrawn but for a day, it would become a frozen rock, rolling lifeless through endless space. So we live in our thoughts and loves. The soul takes wings and flies to the uttermost bounds of space. It disports in infinitude; hope bears it on forever and forever, and love crowns it with joy and gladness. But we forget that, if God withdrew from us but an instant, we should vanish utterly in the inane. The sun is millions of miles away, and yet as close as the throbbings of our hearts; and God seems infinitely remote, but He is in truth the life of our life, and the light of all our ways. If God's being were plain, faith in Him would not be a primary virtue.

If science could make all things intelligible, knowledge would swallow faith here, as St. Paul declares it shall hereafter. But the more we learn, the deeper the mystery grows. Why is knowledge difficult and faith easy? Because faith has the mightier power to impel to action, without which growth is impossible. They who are persuaded that their faith is true, are driven to implant it in the hearts of their children; for they feel that upon the very young alone can the most lasting impressions be made; that what in this tender period is brought home to us as sacred, we shall hardly ever come to look on as profane. The whole world is suffused with the light of those early moods; and religion, rightly learned in childhood, is as fair and full of promise as the dawn, as mellow and soothing as the twilights that gathered about us, while a mother's kisses fell upon our cheeks. Who can doubt that God reveals Himself in the thoughts of the wise and the deeds of the good? A noble mind manifests His wisdom and power in a higher way than the orbs which sparkle in the limitless expanse. Agnosticism which teaches that man can know nothing of the most profoundly interesting subjects, would thereby turn the mind from speculations, which, to take merely this view, have not only the subtlest charm, but the highest educational value. It is by struggling with the unknown, with what, it may be, we cannot know, that we grow in intellectual vigor and suppleness. It is the wrestling of Israel with God, till He bless him. The arguments for the being of God, as distinct from the physical universe, may be logically inconclusive; but the fact remains that the mind is irresistibly driven to look on life, in a godless and soulless world, as a mockery or a curse. We may bear it bravely, may take what it has

to offer with a kind of satisfaction; but we
clearly perceive all the while, that, if the Eternal
is but an idea, life is an affair of hucksters, in
which the profits and pleasures fall below the
expenses and pains; a business whose only possible issue is bankruptcy.

If thou believest in God's love, thou shalt be
slow to believe that any one is excluded from
His boundless sympathy. If not from His,
then not from thine, if thou art His servant.
"When it is asked," says St. Augustine,
"whether one be a good man, there is not
question of what he believes or hopes, but of
what he loves. For he who loves rightly, rightly
believes and rightly hopes; but he who loves
not, believes in vain, hopes in vain." Again:
"Little love is little righteousness; great love is
great righteousness; perfect love is perfect
righteousness." If I should be willing to travel
around the earth to talk with a man of original
insight, I should more gladly make the journey
to open my heart to one who, in spirit even,
had leaned upon the bosom of Christ and known
and felt the infinite love of God. A music-box
plays the works of the great composers, but it
is, after all, only music-box music. So any self-
sufficient man may re-utter the words of Christ;
but spoken by such an one they cease to be
words of light and life. It is not enough that

the sun is the centre of intensest heat; if it is to make a habitable world, it must have a proper medium for the diffusion of its energy. The soul never loses what has been once clearly perceived or deeply felt. In whatever recesses it may lie hidden, it remains for good or evil part of its life, and will, under proper provocation, again emerge in consciousness.

> " One accent of the Holy Ghost
> The heedless world has never lost."

Teach me, O God! to be happy in all the good which thou givest to my fellowmen, in all their joy and striving for better things, in all their sympathy and love, in all their courage and endurance of what is hard to bear.

Credulity is not faith, superstition is not reverence, intolerance is not love of truth, fanaticism is not zeal, and ceremony is not the worship of God in spirit and in truth; but all these things are so blended and commingled in the mind and heart of man that their separation is difficult. Hence the incredulous find faith hard, they who have no superstition easily fail in reverence, they who are without intolerance become indifferent, they who have no piety fall victims to callousness, and they who have no fixed form of worship scarcely worship at all. The best, however, keep careful watch over themselves, lest they confuse means with ends, or be blinded by the apparent to the infinite hidden reality, or permit unworthy passions to obscure the presence of God in the soul. They throw the whole weight of their lives on Him, and strive day by day to draw nearer to Him through obedience, service, and love; seeing Him in all things, and feeling after Him with all the powers of their being.

It is easy to follow a ritual, as it is easy to show that ritualism is insufficient. The beautiful is not the holy, and art is not religion. A pure soul is dearer to God than the splendors of the heavens, than whatever fairest things the hand of man has wrought. But, nevertheless, love will clothe itself with beauty, will find symbols for its worship, in the sun and the stars, and the flowers, and the many tinted shades of light; it will utter itself in melodious sounds and in whatever else speaks of its gladness and exultation, its faith and reverence, its hope and yearning. It will build for itself a tabernacle wherein it may minister with joyful service; and the vesture wherewith it clothes itself shields the flame which is its life. Hence the most genuine and spiritual religion is not found in those who feel no need of a form of worship, but in those who, like the Psalmist, call upon heaven and earth, the mountains and the rivers, the birds

and the beasts and their fellowmen, to join with
them to help them show their love and longing
for God. Religion is love; and love is humble,
reverent, devout, and serviceable. When it does
much, it thinks it little; when it gives all, it
deems it naught. But if the heart is dead, if
the soul has fled, the ceremony is but mockery,
the temple but a tomb; and, in prescribed
observances, there is always a danger lest they
become formal and mechanical, lest we rest in
them; forgetting that, if they are not the expression of living faith and love, they are but
superstitious rites. Whether our suggestions
come from the contemplation of nature or of the
world, from the study of history or the conversations of men, from our own experience or the
dreams of poets, — they will be of many and
often conflicting kinds; and it is for us to choose
which we shall cherish and which we shall reject.
But, if we are wise, we shall receive and hold
those alone which make for strong, brave, and
joyful life; for, since life is the best, the supreme
truth in God Himself, whatever enriches and
purifies life is good; while what weakens and
degrades it is false and hurtful.

CHAPTER II.

THOUGHTS AND THEORIES.

In life's fair garden still there are
So many plots which fallow lie,
So many flowers which soon will die
Unless true workers death's steps bar.

And each of us may also find
In his own heart so many a spot
Where truth and love are cherished not,
To blank indifference resigned.

EDUCATION is mightier than man; in other words, evolution, directed by conscious will, is capable of doing more than any man is capable of becoming. Believe, then, in education; and let thy faith give thee confidence in thyself when thou strivest to upbuild thy being. The young ask with impatience how long it will take to finish their education; the wise are happy in the knowledge that while life lasts theirs cannot end. Faith in what we do can alone guide us to perfect work. Who shall forbid a man to help his fellowman? Who, then, shall forbid him to teach, to educate? To communicate facts is easy; but the educator's business is to create dispositions, and this is difficult. His aim is not to make learning easy, but to accustom the pupil to labor, since nothing but a man's own industry can develop his faculties or give him strength and grasp of mind; and this, and not mere knowing, is the end of education. The teacher's main purpose is to form habits of industry, which will assert themselves, not in the school alone, but in the home as well; for unless the young are trained to study at home, they will soon cease to study at all; and this means degeneracy or ruin. The teacher who knows his business, and is at the same time industrious and morally blameless, can accomplish incredible things if he give himself wholly to his task. Like all true workers he does the best he can, for love of the work; as a mother devotes herself, looking for no other reward than the character her life and counsels shall form in her child. Faith in love, in its worth as the great humanizing power, makes the mother the highest earthly source of education; and it is the characteristic of all genuine teachers. "Love," says Pestalozzi, "is the only, the eternal foundation of the training of our race to humanity." "Love," says Goethe, "does not rule, but it educates, and this is more." The educator is an enthusiast, not noisy or shallow, but deep and self-impelled. His ideal is that of human perfection. He is in love with noble

men and women, and he feels that it is a joy
to be alive when one is permitted to labor to
bring forth the divine image in himself and in
others.

To think of education as a means of preserv-
ing institutions, however excellent, is to form
a wrong conception of its purpose, which is to
mould and fashion men, who are more than
institutions, who create, outgrow, and recreate
institutions. Education concerns every one, not
for the reason chiefly that it is a matter of vital
general interest, having an immediate bearing
on the welfare and progress of every people and
of the whole race; but because each one, if he
is to become a true man, must make his own
education his life work, to which whatever he
undertakes or does or suffers, must be auxiliary.
It is, therefore, a subject not for philosophers
and schoolmasters, for parents and citizens
alone, but for whoever cherishes his human
nature, or aspires to perfection, which is attainable only through the development of the faculties wherewith God has endowed him. Every
man, therefore, should be an educator, — an
educator of himself; and how shall he hope to
perform this task wisely, if he remain ignorant
of what education means and requires. The
matter, indeed, seems to be simple, — but is
deep as heaven, as wide as the world, and as

complex as life. It is the art of right living,
the science of whatever influences man. The
knowledge which we acquire from a desire for
knowledge, enters into our mental life and becomes an enduring part of ourselves; while
what we learn from vanity or emulation, or as
a means to a livelihood, does not form character
or remain as a permanent gain. Education is a
process of life-development. Life is developed
by nutrition and exercise. The teacher's business, therefore, is to rouse in the pupil a desire
for spiritual nourishment and to supply him
with it in a way which will impel him to self-
activity.

What does a wise teacher strive to develop in
his scholars? Ability, the power to grapple
with whatever questions and difficulties, to face
whatever temptations and sufferings, and to
overcome them by doing and bearing; or, shall
I say, that it is his aim to give insight into the
meaning and worth of life, and to form the
faculties whereby man asserts himself as an intelligent, moral, and religious being. Learning
about things is of small importance; while to
learn to use the senses, and to turn the mind
on things, is all-important. The young, to be
deeply roused, require spiritual ideals; and
they are fortunate when, in the light of these
ideals, they are led to understand what is prac-

tical, that their enthusiasm for the good and the great may be sustained by delight in their work.

There are few words more abused than "enthusiasm," which, when rightly understood, is one of the best we have. As the Greeks used it, it meant the state of one who is possessed and inspired by a god. It implied, therefore, the gathering of all the powers of the soul into a higher unity, and the turning them, with intenser energy, whether to contemplation or to action. In this sense it is the symbol of a mental or moral condition, which is indispensable to the achievement of aught that is excellent. It alone supplies the impulse which steadies the view, fixes the thought, and leads to life-long labor for the accomplishment of a worthy purpose. It does not manifest itself in ebullitions of sentiment or rhetoric; it is a deep glowing fire rather than a flame; it utters itself in deeds more than in words. It makes one capable of infinite patience and endurance, and holds him true in the face of whatever difficulties, — steadfast, though a world cry out against him. It is what Christ sought in his disciples; and what, above all else, he demanded of them as the natural and necessary result of a living hope, faith, and love. To understand a word we should know its history; be able to trace it

4

to the mother-root from which it first sprang, and to follow it through all its variations of form and meaning. So long as we continue to accept words as purely conventional signs, we cannot come to true insight. They are the vesture the soul of man has woven for itself; the form and body of its experience in the world; the organ wherewith it utters itself and becomes conscious of its life. To treat them as something agreed upon is to miss their power and beauty. As children we all receive them in an unthinking way; and, unless we recreate our language for ourselves, our minds remain childish.

It is the radical fault of our institutions of learning, that, while they teach many things, they leave the mind and character unformed. Their graduates are able to tell us about philosophy, poetry, and science, but they take no delight in the use of their faculties; and hence, like Indians, who, having learned something of civilized life, return to their tribes but to sink back into the old ways, our young men, when they quit college, abandon all thought of self-improvement, and are soon lost in the crowd; while others who have not had their opportunities, but are self-impelled, keep at work and rise to distinction. The educational value of the knowledge acquired at school is determined by its effect on the pupil's will. If this is roused and urged onward to whatever is true and good, the teacher's chief work is done. Suns and planets contend with one another, attracting and repelling; atoms with atoms, elements with elements; and in the animal world there is ceaseless pursuing and fleeing, struggle and battle, as among men there is rivalry, contention, and war between races, nations, classes, cities, families, and individuals. Nay, within each one's breast the combat rages, as though angels and demons fought for the soul. Thou must defend thy life or lose it. Some thought of this kind was in the mind of Malebranche, when he said if he held Truth captive in his hand, he would let it fly, that he might be impelled to its pursuit; and Lessing has expressed the same sentiment in slightly different words.

" The little quickly vanishes from view
    Of him who sees how much remains to do."

The study of biographies, which contain the history of the intellectual and moral growth of those who have nobly striven to improve themselves, is an effective means of education, and much to be commended to the young who desire to distinguish themselves by personal worth and useful deeds. It may be that in this our but feebly creative time, the best service one can render is to inspire a love of the best books. It is safe to say that nine-tenths of the story books written for children, are worthless or harmful; and the periodical child-literature is also as a rule foolish and false. Better to play or sleep or perform any idle task than to read such things. Boys and girls who read the daily newspapers are doomed. They may not all become idle or vicious, but none of them will become noble or great. As well expect them to attain bodily health and vigor on a diet of gin and doughnuts. Stories and poetry are the best for them; but they should be works of genius or lives of real men, who suffered, toiled, and struggled; who, in the midst of whatever kind of mishaps, failures, and dangers, kept true to their purpose, continuing to labor and to hope. The young think of life as an opportunity for enjoyment or for improving one's position in the world, never turning their thoughts to its true purpose and use, — the upbuilding of character, the cultivation of the mind, the refinement of the taste, the subduing of selfish and sensual passions, and the seeking for truth, righteousness, and love. Truth, when deeply felt as being one with beauty and goodness, utters itself rhythmically and becomes poetry, which is music also ; for in its highest moods, the soul is melodious, — its faculties, no longer separate, blend to express themselves in divine symphonies. Poetry, therefore, appeals to the whole man, the intellect, the imagination, and the heart. It multiplies joys, soothes in sorrow, strengthens in trial, opens the eye to the boundless wealth and beauty of the world, gives a higher sense of the worth of life, and makes us more conscious of God's presence in the soul. No kind of life is pleasant to him who has not the spirit whereby it may be enjoyed; and as there are many who see no beauty in nature, so there are many who take no delight in books. If thou will but read true and noble words and repeat them to thyself day by day, high thoughts will grow into them and fill them, as the mind interfuses itself with the eye or tongue or hand which is kept worthily occupied.

Advice which enters into details is rarely useful and can hardly be rightly given, since no one can know another, except in a large and general way. Besides, they who need minute direction are children. It is best to commend whoever seeks thy counsel, to put his faith in whatever things are true or good or beautiful, as being the nearest symbols of God, and to strive to come close to them by observation, reflection, reading, prayer, and work, persevered in through life. This is the

plain rule of life: Find and do the highest
work of which thou art capable. How shalt
thou find it? By doing with all thy heart that
which lies at hand. Perseverance, industry,
and labor accomplish more than genius; they
are the elements which make its life possible.
When Ruskin was told that a certain man was a
genius, he simply asked: Does he work? For
whoever loves purely or strives bravely or does
honest work, life's current bears fresh and
fragrant thoughts. His pulse-beats are rhyth-
mical with the courses of the planets; and in his
deepest heart he hears as in echo the songs
of celestial spirits hymning the blessedness of
immortal souls. Forget thyself, forget thy
little pains and miseries, and address thy mind
to truth and thy heart to love, and thou shalt
understand that God is here; that the flowers
look up to Him and laugh; that the waters
feel His presence and are glad, and that the
atoms all thrill at His touch. Be not frightened,
like a child when the door is shut, because He
hides behind the veil; but occupy thyself with
what is good, and when thy task is done,
He will show Himself. He who grows old,
still learning, finds that the years grow shorter,
and he would, were it possible, stay them in
their flight; but to the youth in college they
seem unending, and he would gladly see them

shrink to weeks or days. Why? He who grows old, still learning, takes delight in his work; whereas the youth studies unwillingly, accepting his task in the spirit of a slave, and looking upon himself as a prisoner, longing to be set free. " If," says Ruskin, "there is any one point which in six thousand years of thinking about right and wrong, wise and good men have agreed upon, or successively by experience discovered, it is that God dislikes idle and cruel people more than any other; that His first order is, Work while you have light, and His second, Be merciful while you have mercy."

The whole aim and purpose of the educator is to foster life, to so deal with each individual as to increase his power of life and to heighten his quality of life; and hence in giving instruction he considers chiefly its life-nourishing and life-improving efficacy. There is an outer and an inner knowledge. The former is that of children and thoughtless persons, who know only about things. The inner belongs to those who have wrought their intuitions and experiences, together with whatever information they have received, into the substance of their life. What we teach ourselves gives the purest joy and best nourishes the mind. Once we have gotten some insight into this power of self-vivification, which each one might have, we come of age, learn to create our world wherein we become truth-loving and love-worthy. As it is a father's glory to find in his son a nobler kind of being than he himself is, so is the true educator made happy when he is able to call forth in his pupil a higher humanity than that which he himself possesses. Teacher, educate thyself. In bending with a brave heart to this life-task, thou shalt find not only guidance and illumination in thy work for others, but an unfailing source of enthusiasm, without which thou canst not be a former of immortal souls, but merely a hearer and exactor of lessons; not a sower of the seed of truth and love, but a grinder of corn which can never take root and bear a hundred fold.

Like priest, like people; like teacher, like pupil. We acquire the virtues of our friends and the vices of our enemies; but as vice is easy and virtue difficult, we are more apt to be corrupted by those with whom we contend than to be improved by those we love. In the teacher we require not only a cultivated mind, but a complete man, — wise, estimable, brave, generous, and, above all, loving. As the race advances in knowledge and power, education becomes more many-sided and difficult; but it becomes, also, more indispensable; for the demands made upon the individual become more urgent and manifold. Whatever goes to the making of a man is subject to the law of development, and may, therefore, be educated, — body and soul, mind and heart, spirit and disposition, inclination and will, which are all intertwined and interdependent. And hence the teacher must direct his thought to them all, for, as Montaigne says, it is not a body or a soul, but a man that he has to educate. Since education is essentially self-education, the teacher has little more to do than to guide the pupil in the art and practice of self-vivification. He who strives unwearyingly to make himself more knowing, more loving, and more helpful, becomes conscious of ever-increasing inner strength and joy. Wise and happy in himself, he will draw others to him to inspire and bless them with higher thoughts and nobler courage. He alone who feels that to form and cultivate himself is an ever-present duty, is conscious of a vocation to work for the education of others. No one does well who is not impelled by faith in the worth of what he does; and he who has faith in education must show it first of all by the efforts which he makes to improve himself. We are all under the formative influences of Nature, reason, and God; and the more consciously and fully we yield to these influences, the higher do we rise in dignity of being.

Thoroughness of knowledge and consummate skill are not the only ends of education. We have, besides the faculty of knowing, the faculties of willing, loving, hoping, and believing; besides intellect and physical strength, we have imagination and conscience; and all these must be cultivated if we are to form a true man. Principle has higher worth than knowledge, and a loving heart is better than much gold. Genuine education is that which trains to godliness and virtue, to truthfulness and the love of spiritual beauty; for this makes a man, and all else is incidental. Popular ideals are never true ideals; and it is the business of the educator to lead his pupils to a knowledge of higher things than those the crowd seeks. While he inculcates patriotism he must hold their minds and hearts close to the eternal principles, which make all men akin and citizens of God's state. The higher we rise the more we feel ourselves men, and the less we think of ourselves as belonging to a party or a nation. The best patriot is he who is most truly a man.

Public opinion is made up of truth and error, and it is the business of the wise to separate the genuine from the false. There is nothing either so fair or so useful as a knowing and loving man; and therefore, the education which best helps to form such an one is in every way the most desirable. We know the history of education, even in its minute details; but when we come to establish a system of our own, we waver, disagree, and grope helplessly; and the outcome seems to be that no people has ever taught so much or educated so little. Love, filial piety, devoutness, sympathy, gentleness, patience, courage, obedience, serviceableness, and chastity are not the fruits of intellectual culture, but may be found in greater purity in simple hearts than in learned minds.

Dost thou think it desirable to be born rich, or to attain political or commercial distinction and influence? Canst thou not see that they who are born rich, or who attain political or commercial distinction, rarely become true men, but lack the best insight and the highest virtue? Be thankful, then, for what in thy youth thou didst hold to be disadvantages and obstacles; for to them thou owest thy vocation to the pursuit of knowledge and the striving for excellence. But the smallest part of self emerges in consciousness; and the relation of our subconscious life to God and our fellowmen has a more important bearing on character than anything we understand. To imagine, then, that we educate when we do nothing but sharpen the intellect is a shallow conceit. Wiser than the knowing are they who feel God's presence and man's sacredness, and who walk in reverence and in lowliness of spirit.

Once we have acquired the habit of inner attention, a thousand truths come to us without our seeking. Life develops from within, and he who would educate must work upon the soul. Duty, honor, liberty, reason, culture, progress, truth, and love are thought values. We cannot see, hear, taste, smell, or touch them. Are they, therefore, abstractions and illusions? Are they not rather the most real of things, — the life of our life and the soul of our being? A wise mother acquaints herself with proverbs, and lets them drop in due season, like ripe seed, into the hearts of her children. She will also sing to them old songs, full of aspiration and yearning, of faith in what is high and true; and she will read short poems to them, but only the best. Let her, then, be a good reader as well as a sweet singer.

It seems doubtful whether a woman who cannot sing and who does not love poetry, has the right to marry. If she have no music in herself, how shall she learn to be a mother? How shall she touch the hidden springs of harmony which lie within the souls of children? If we did but take these little ones to our hearts in the spirit of the Divine Saviour, we might form a race of men who would establish the

Kingdom of God on earth. What we all require as the indispensable condition of healthful growing life is vital sympathy with God, with our family, with our people, with the whole human brotherhood. But the world grasps us, in our youth, with a thousand hands, to shape us after its own fashion; and it is miraculous if one escape, and in the pure air of study and all noble effort, rise heavenward.

Learn to look, to listen, to hear, and to exercise thyself, and thou shalt soon perceive that earth is but a training ground whereon God has placed thee that thou mayst grow strong, wise, and good. None of us fathom the meaning of the words of the Saviour. " They have eyes and see not, ears and hear not." If we would but look and listen within and without, we should quickly know that God is with us, and that all He asks us to do is to love and to grow. Be persuaded, in thy deepest heart, that there is no individual, no people, no race, that is not worthy to be loved and educated, rather than to be scorned and held in darkness and bondage.

In 1725, a party of hunters found a youth, of about fifteen years, in the woods, near Hamelin, Germany. He was naked, ran on all fours, swung himself, like a monkey, from tree to tree, and ate moss and grass. When he was caught and taken to England, he tore off the clothes that were put on him and continued to devour his food raw. The king placed him under the tuition of Dr. Arbuthnot; but, though he lived to be seventy, he never learned to talk.

In 1687, a boy about twelve years old was discovered, living with beasts, in the forest of Grodno, Russia. He was captured and taken to Warsaw. His hair was very thick and white, his fingers long, his forehead of average dimension, and his voice like the growl of a bear. He ran on all fours, and it was with much difficulty that he was taught to walk upright, though his physical development was perfect. He ate grass, and was fond of raw meat and vegetables. It took much time and trouble to teach him to utter articulate sounds, and violence had to be used to get him to wear clothes.

In 1731, a girl, about ten years old, appeared in the village of Songi, in Champagne, France. She was barefooted, and her body was covered with rags and pieces of hide. In her hand she held a club, and when a dog rushed at her, she stood firm, and with a single blow laid him dead at her feet. She then fled into the fields, climbed a tree, and soon fell asleep. Having been induced to descend and enter a neighboring castle, she strangled a rabbit which was handed to her and ate it raw. She was of robust constitution, and her thumbs were exceptionally strong, due doubtless to her habit of climbing. She sprang with ease from tree to tree; and was so quick that she caught birds on the wing, or plunging into the water seized fishes, which she at once devoured. She could not speak, but emitted only inarticulate sounds. These are examples of what we should all be were it not for education.

Pleasure springs from the satisfaction of desire. The craving for food is universal: so, therefore, is the pleasure of eating; but this man has in common with the brute. His humanity appears with the desire for what is spiritual, for truth, freedom, beauty, and righteousness. The animal appetites are soon appeased; and then they leave us sluggish, until hunger or thirst or sexual desire rouse us again. The pleasure their gratification gives is heavy and monotonous. Hence they who live in the sensual nature soon exhaust what is to be found there, and become victims of satiety and *ennui*. To escape from themselves they go into company, take refuge in pastimes, assist at spectacles, or travel in foreign lands. But what exile from himself can flee? Wherever they go, whatever they do, they bear with them the weight of their animalism, and drag the lengthening chain of their slavish passions.

There is no redemption for them, unless we can awaken in them the desire for what is spiritual, for truth, freedom, beauty, and righteousness.

Intellectual delight, the joy there is in simply knowing a thing, is tasted by few; but they who are insensible to this pleasure lack impulse to the exercise of mind which makes culture possible. For them ignorance is not suffering, and mental effort is pain. Why should the daily happenings interest and occupy thee, if in themselves they are unimportant? A week hence they will be forgotten. Why then let them rob thee now of the time which, rightly employed, would make thee wise and strong? Children may run to the window to watch the flight of an insect; but why should men and women allow their time and strength to be dissipated by the noise of gossip, by tales of trifles signifying nothing? Thought prospers best in solitude; but the thinker is alone in the midst of crowds. To know how to improve and correct with skill and tact, in the spirit of kindly tolerance, the judgments, appreciations, and surmises of the young, is to be able to render them important service, since in this way they may best be taught to see things as they are, and to think for themselves. All teaching is a demonstration, a leading to the right point of view, while we say, Now look, and tell me what you see.

What we do not see ourselves we never see at all; for, even when we look through the eyes of another, it is with our own that we see. In the home, in the school, in the church, and in the State, the individual is taught that it is necessary to have regard not to himself alone, but to the whole body of which he is a member. If he prefer himself to the general welfare, he is made to feel that his private good is attainable only in the community, that it can be well with him only when it is well with those with whom he lives and is associated. Hence in the home and the school, as in the larger organisms, there should be no privilege, no partiality; otherwise the sense of order and justice is offended. In this way alone can we train the young to obedience, attention, respect, and politeness. They are far less impressed by what they hear us say than by what they see us do. They are all eyes, and words have for them but vague meanings.

Since the mother teaches the child her language, how is it possible not to impart the living content of her speech, — her faith, love, and religion? If in the home this inner education is neglected, no real education is given there. We can educate for a larger environment only by teaching the young to adapt themselves to one which is smaller. The home should educate for the school, the school for the church and the State, the church and the State for the human race and God. A fondness for slang is a characteristic of crude minds or of the degenerate. The correct use of language springs from right thinking and right feeling. But if we are to speak our mother tongue with propriety and grace, our mothers must be our teachers. The home is the fountain-head of English pure and undefiled. Language is the motherhouse and fatherland of the mind. It is the body which it must nourish, exercise, and get control of, that it may itself possess vigor and suppleness. Things reveal themselves in distinctness only when they are clothed in words. Our knowledge floats from us like dissolving vapors unless we imprison it in speech. The name is wedded to the thing, and the union is inviolable. We think in words, and without them our perceptions are rudimentary, our ideas unreal, our opinions inarticulate. Verbal utterance expresses the mind as the countenance reveals the soul. It is a currency whose value is everywhere recognized. It is the bond which knits individuals into wholes, in the family, in the church, in the State. It is the music which we most love to hear, whether it greet us from the lips of children, of maidens, and of youths, or rise like organ-tones from the breasts of orators and the hearts of poets, or whisper in the gentle voices of mothers and lovers, or fall like echoes from eternal worlds, when believing souls pour their orisons to God. It winds itself about the thousand little things which make our human life, and widens to embrace the universe, bringing it close to the mind of man. It lends itself to all colors and forms; adapts itself to all moods; is tender or harsh or weak or strong. It interprets the voice of the thunder, the dreams of the night, the gladness of the stars, the dawn's shout of victory. It is the vesture which the soul has woven for itself, taking invisible atoms and moulding them into sounds which mediate between the seen and the unseen, the finite and the infinite. In the works of genius, where it is found in perfection, it is a mirror wherein the mind sees itself, not in isolation and nakedness, but in the marvellous setting in which God has placed it in the midst of His Universe. It is not merely the instrument, the sole instrument, I may say, wherewith our own thoughts can be rightly expressed and those of others made intelligible; but it is the one means by which we are made conscious of what we think and love. It is more wonderful than the celestial harmonies of which poets dream. Learn to treat it with respect, and speak no false or harsh or mutilated word.

Children understand what is base better than what is simply wrong; and an effectual way to turn them from vice is to show them that it is degrading, as the Spartans brought drunken Helots before their youths to fill them with disgust for what they grew accustomed to consider a vice of a servile race. Let the young be made to feel that ignorance is a gross and animal thing, that lying and deceit are cowardly and ignoble, that careless work is dishonest and waste of time, sheer idiocy. It is a mistake to weary children with lessons of morality and religion; for, if they once get a distaste for such truth, it will hardly be possible to impress them with a sense of its importance. We educate morally when we hold the pupil to what is right, and accustom him to do what duty commands. Character is moulded by deeds, not by doctrines. The habit of facing danger makes the veteran braver than the raw recruit; the habit of facing truth makes the philosopher wiser than the boor; the habit of facing conscience makes the saint holier than the worldling; the habit of facing beauty gives the poet diviner insight than the common man may have; the habit of labor, in whatever sphere, is the source of excellence. We do not naturally love work; for work is effort, and effort is painful. We, therefore, have to be educated to work; and to teach the young to labor in obedience to the voice of duty is one of the main purposes for which the school exists. Hence unless it is to become a place of perversion, it must be a realm of order, punctuality, obedience, and industry, where attention and interest are kept constantly awake. In such a school, work grows to be a habit; and delight in work is the result. Sloth is a radical vice, — it bars the way to the exercise of our higher faculties in every direction; it is the chief obstacle in the path of progress of all kinds. We do well only what we do with our whole heart; and the teacher's work lacks the best quality unless he loves his calling and works gladly therein. The heart makes the orator, and it makes the teacher too. It is a weakness in our present life that few work with a cheerful and contented spirit at the tasks they have chosen. Whatever his occupation or vocation, each one has his thought upon more money or higher place or a larger city to dwell in, and is therefore restless. He loses the good of life in striving for life's accompaniments.

To nearly all of us who succeed a little the devil sends tempters in the guise of friends to whisper that our worth is not recognized, as though title or position could be other than a burden and hindrance for those who live within themselves and have real merit. The teacher, who, having a competency, turns his attention to an increase of salary, has nothing of the true educator's enthusiasm. A physician or a lawyer who possesses exceptional skill may be forced in self-defence to make his fees large; but money cannot secure the service of the best teachers, for other things are of more importance to them; freedom, for instance, and leisure, and the spirit of the institution in which they labor. The genius of the spot affects them. Their wants are few, their tastes inexpensive; and they easily prefer a small to a large city, because its atmosphere is more favorable to recollection and study, to mental and moral growth.

"When I hear Socrates," said Alcibiades, "my heart leaps higher than the Corybants, and my eyes fill with tears; and I see that he affects others in the same way. I tear myself from him with violence and flee, holding my ears, as from the Songs of Sirens, lest I grow old sitting there listening to him." To meet with such a teacher is the best fortune which can fall to the young, as the worst is to be delivered up to mechanical and pedantic minds by whom their spiritual being is blighted.

To know how to teach, to teach well, — this is the schoolmaster's whole business. If he teach well he will also live well, since only a good man can have the disinterested love of truth and of human perfection, which makes right teaching possible. Good teachers and good teaching educate; bad teachers and bad teaching benumb, warp, and pervert. This is the sum of all our pedagogical science and art. They who neglect to educate themselves would, if they were not shameless as well as ignorant, make no pretence to be friends and lovers of education. The teacher should be what he desires to help his pupils to become; yet must he not be a finished man, but a learner and striver. Not a poem or a statue or a painting, not a philosophy or a science or a political constitution, is the highest achievement of man; the noblest work of man is a noble man.

When Antipater demanded of the Spartans fifty of their youths as hostages, they offered him instead a hundred of their principal men, being willing to make any sacrifice rather than deprive their children of the advantages of Spartan training. They could have given no better proof of their love of country or of their faith in its institutions. What a man genuinely believes to be the best, he strives to provide for his children, whether it be money or culture or religion. They can hardly be said to have faith

who feel not an irresistible impulse to transmit
to their descendants what they believe to be the
highest and the holiest. Education is an art
more than it is a scientific theory; and, unless
one is born with talent for an art, study will not
enable him to pursue it with more than mod-
erate success. The number of born teachers,
however, is not great; and nothing is left us
but to train, as best we may, those who lack
power to interest, to command attention, and
to create enthusiasm. Socrates sent a youth
back to his father, saying: " I can teach him
nothing, he does not love me." Whatever
we teach, the young should be clothed in
beauty. They delight in sunlight and flowers,
their hearts leap forth to all fair and happy
things; and though we may compel them to
accept, we can never make them love what is
harsh or gloomy. The stronger the personality of the teacher, the more disposed will he
be to concede them freedom, contenting himself with being their leader. Tyranny is the
result of fear, of the fear which wrong and cru-
elty beget in their author, or of the fear which
is born of the tyrant's consciousness of his
weakness. To make a man we must risk the
spoiling of a youth.

" Before each one an image floats of what he ought to be,
  And till he this attains, his life is never full and free."

As Socrates was walking with some of his disciples in the gardens of Pericles, the conversation turned upon art and its divine beauties. " Tell us," said Alcibiades, with a smile, " tell us, O Socrates! how thou camest to make the statues of the Graces; and why, having finished thy masterpiece, thou didst abandon art. Would thou hadst given us also the goddess of Wisdom!" "I will relate," replied Socrates, " the story of my art, and thou shalt then decide, Alcibiades, whether it would be well for me again to grasp the mallet and chisel. As a youth I loved art with all my heart, and was accustomed to visit the workshops of the masters and the temples of the gods; for in those I hoped to receive instruction, and in these divine enthusiasm. With this view I went one day to a little temple on the boundary of Attica, dedicated to the Graces. The simplicity of its form invited me, and I said to myself, ' Though thou find nothing for thy art — for how could a marble statue have strayed hither? — yet mayest thou nourish and cultivate here a taste for simplicity,' since this, as I thought, should not be lacking in an artist. At the door of the little temple an old man of venerable and friendly countenance met me. ' What seekest thou here, my son?' he inquired with a gentle voice. I told him that I was an art-student, and

that I had sought the temple to improve myself.
' It is well, my son,' he replied, ' that thou be-
ginnest with thyself and approachest the godlike to produce it in thyself, before thou at-
temptest to body it forth. Thy efforts shall
not go unrewarded. I will show thee what else-
where in all Greece thou shouldst look for in
vain, — the first and oldest statues of the Graces.'
Thereupon he pointed to three square rough-
hewn stones, and said : ' Behold, there they
are.' I looked at him and was silent. But he
smiled and continued : ' Dost thou find it strange
that the godlike should have been in the heart
of man before his tongue or his hand could give
it expression? Well, show thy reverence for it,
by endowing it with a worthier form. I am the
priest of this temple ; my duty calls me now.'
He went, and left me in an unwonted mood.
Returning to Athens, I made the statues of the
Graces. You know them. I took them to the
priest as an offering for the temple, and pre-
sented them to him with a trembling hand.
' Well done, my son,' said the friendly old man ;
' thou hast accomplished thy task with industry
and zeal. But,' he continued, with a serious
air, ' tell me, hast thou also satisfied thyself?'
' Alas ! no,' I replied ; ' I have a nobler image in
my soul, to which I feel that the hand is powerless
to give form.' The venerable man laid his hand

upon my shoulder and spoke with indescribable grace. 'Well, then, take thy statues to the halls of the rich men of Athens, and leave us our stones. We, my son, in our simplicity, have faith, and the plainest symbol suffices; but they have only knowledge, and, therefore, need the work of art. To thee I give this counsel: Learn to know the divine germ which lies in thee and in every human heart; cherish it, and thou shalt produce the godlike within and without thyself.' He left me, and I returned with my statues, meditating the words of the old man, who appeared to me to be a god. I stood a whole night beneath the stars, and as the sun rose it became clear within my soul also. I recognized the eternal Grace, Love, within and without myself. I prayed, hastened home, laid my mallet and chisel at the feet of my statues of the Graces, and, coming forth, found you, my dear friends and disciples. Are ye not the noblest expression of the divine Grace; and shall I not live longer in such images than in cold fragile marble?"

> A free soul only grows not old,
> For he lives in worlds unseen,
> Where stealthy time can take no hold
> Nor dim fair Beauty's sheen.

It is not effort, but fruitless effort, which makes work distasteful; and if the teacher but

show his pupils how to use their powers rightly,
they will apply themselves to their tasks as
gladly as bees to their honey-making. Happy
children make happy men and women. Oh!
sadden not the souls that have just budded
from out the bosom of God. It is easy, however, to carry too far the notion that everything
should be made pleasant for the young. Education is for life; and in life much that a man
has to do cannot be made pleasant, but must
be done from a sense of duty. Indeed, a great
part of the teacher's business is to accustom
pupils to do what they do not like to do. The
larger a people's political, social, and religious
liberty, the more perfect should be the discipline of its schools. The child who breaks a
rule through heedlessness should be punished;
for it is the business of education to teach him
the necessity of giving heed. Inattention is
a radical fault in school as in life. Will creates
will, and many words enfeeble it. Live the
life, but utter thy thoughts about it briefly,
feeling that they need little expression other
than thy behavior. To be able to guide the
pupil's will, the teacher must gain possession
of his heart. But the young give themselves
to those alone whose genuine good-will towards
them they are certain of. As water is infinitely
more valuable to man than gold, since the one

is essential to his life, while the other is but a standard of value or an ornament, so is love worth infinitely more to him than knowledge; since love is his life, while knowledge is chiefly a means whereby it may be preserved and enriched. Hence the educator who rouses his pupils to the love of what is true, good, and fair, renders higher service than the teacher who sharpens the intellect or imparts information. We easily content ourselves with little where no one has much. It is the contrast that disturbs us. In the presence of the rich we feel our poverty; where all are ignorant, none are conscious of their lack of knowledge. Education, like religion, art, and science, is appreciated by those alone who are convinced of its surpassing worth, and who seriously strive to bring their lives into harmony with its principles. He who believes, with all his heart, in truth as the supreme good, and who follows after it day by day, will find peace and increase of life. There is no need to ask that it be useful, or bring anything else than the possession of itself. They alone are nobly contented whose hours are so filled with the work which they love, that, in doing it, they forget to think of themselves.

A brave, manly character, enrooted in rational ideas and convictions, is the fine outcome of a liberal education. Let us teach the young the great harmonic truths and beliefs by which we ourselves have been made human, and pass lightly over errors, disputes, divisions, and hatreds. Let it be our aim to make them men of good-will, not partisans. Strive not to determine them to this or that vocation, but so educate them that they shall be able to make intelligent choice of their life-work. Tame first the beast in man, that reason and conscience may emerge. Then cultivate reason and conscience, that intellectual and moral strength may be developed. He who having accomplished worthy things still ponders how he may upbuild his being and achieve something yet nobler, heedless of the world's censure or applause, is a great man. Virtue is a quality of strength; and the wise are distrustful of the seeming virtues of the weak. If the end of education be virtue, whatever enfeebles is contrary to its purpose. The young are not made brave and hardy by being told that they ought to be so, but by being thrown into surroundings which try and thereby develop their courage and endurance. To talk about what one does not care for can do little good. Only they teach well who are thoroughly in earnest, and thoroughly interested in their work. From the best, everything good may be obtained by confidence and frankness. Think not of what harm thou mightst do to another, but only of what good. To feel that whatever wise and helpful thing thou canst do, thou shouldst do; and to accept the task thus set thee by God, with a cheerful and willing heart, as the brave gladly hold the post of danger, — this is happiness; yea, this is blessedness. They who are drawn to study, not by motives of utility, but by dis-interested sympathy, derive the purest benefits. Studies, pursued with a view to the material gain to be gotten from them, in the practice of a profession, for instance, are called by the Germans "bread studies." They do little to open and illumine the mind; and where the learned are almost exclusively bread-study men, an enlightened public, one that loves thought for its own sake, is necessarily lacking.

In the presence of human indolence and in-difference, God himself seems to be helpless. Whether we speak or whether we write, let the one aim be to stir our own minds and those of our hearers and readers toward the best things. Let the teacher be joyful, serious, and inexo-rable. It is impossible to know and love chil-dren without feeling that right education would enable us, in a single generation, to bring into existence a higher kind of man than has hitherto lived. We spoil them not only by our false spirit and mechanical methods, but by wrong treatment of many kinds; so that in the end they are made as dull, selfish, and insincere as we are. Thy law must be good through good; not good through evil. But if evil befall, convert it to good, by wringing from it deeper wisdom and higher courage. Let truth and justice be thy weapons. Yield not to the brute passion which would render evil for evil; but know that reason and con-science are stronger than material forces, the quality of their strength being supreme and permanent. It is that within the soul which is likest unto God. Culture is not merely a development of endowments; it is the awaken-ing of the soul from the sleep of the senses to a consciousness of God's presence. Of how little of the infinite reality the most knowing mind is conscious! There is room for thee to grow in knowledge and love throughout eternity. Let the good stand in the front ranks. If they flee from the battle-field, the wicked will triumph. The world is ruled by minorities who have defi-nite aims and conscious purposes.

It is only by rising out of time that we can bring back the past, live in it, feel its power, and learn the lessons it has to teach. The history of institutions has both a real and a sentimental value; but the important consideration always is what they now are, and what they now and here are able to do for the spiritual life of men. Few really believe. The most only believe that they believe or even make believe. In this absence of faith, ideals lose meaning; and thought and action come to seem illusory. They who do well habitually have neither time nor inclination to talk about themselves or their work. Thou hast accomplished little; but thou shalt never accomplish anything by thinking how little thou hast done. To educate a human being is to nourish and guide with knowledge and skill the powers of his life, that, as his faculties become perfected, he may employ them for worthy ends; it is to form in him, while he is yet young, the disposition which will be useful and necessary to him when he is grown, that he may become accustomed, while his reason is yet undeveloped, to love and hate what he ought to love and hate. The will to live is the radical impulse ; and the aim of education is to confirm, enlighten, and purify the will to live, — the will to live in God and in humanity. One's talent and temperament indicate what he may become; his way of thinking shows what he wishes to make of himself. A vulgar expression is doubly offensive when uttered by lips which seem made to speak only what is filled with the light of truth and love. What the individual, left to himself, could not accomplish, though he lived for centuries, education does for him in a few years. German philological scholarship has ruined German literature, — has cast a blight on all literature. It has led the modern mind to analyze and dissect literature, until sense for that which makes literature a vital force has been enfeebled or lost.

When we have listened in pedagogical institutes and educational conventions to the stream of talk about methods in the study of literature, we remember with thankfulness, that, when we were young, one could take his Shakspere with him into the woods, and hear him sing as he heard the birds sing, in blissful ignorance of all this learning and methodology. The great purpose of poetry is to inspire, of history to create, enthusiasm, and what we ask of the teacher, above all things, is that he inspire and create enthusiasm. But whether he shall do this depends not on the words he speaks but on the life he lives. When some one asked Zeuxidamus why the Lacedæmonians did not reduce their rules for education to writing that the young might read them, he replied: " Because they wished to accustom their youths to deeds, not to words." Pythagoras bade his disciples be silent, or speak what is better than silence.

A microbe, floating invisible in the dust of a room, may destroy the life of a man; a fault, so slight as scarcely to be noticeable, may grow until it ruins all. A wise word may give the impulse which starts a youth on a career of honor and beneficence. Linné, the first of botanists, was considered so dull that his father took him from school and apprenticed him to a shoemaker. A physician noticing with what patience he gathered plants in the fields and woods, declared there was in him the making of a naturalist; and he was consequently permitted to follow the bent of his genius. It is a chance if one who is not intellectually and morally active is not reduced to drudgery and wretchedness. If thou wouldst be safe, be a man, — wise, strong, and helpful. The choice of a vocation is of minor importance to him, who, understanding that life is given him that he may upbuild his being on the foundation of truth and love, is resolved to devote all his energies to the divinely imposed task. Have patience with every one, and with thyself first of all. We can help men only by making them better; and we can improve society only by improving men. Each one is himself his own good or bad fortune.

"Duty! wonderful thought!" says Kant, "thou workest not by persuasion or flattery, nor yet by threats; but thou holdest thy naked law before the soul, and compellest respect, though not always obedience; so that all lusts, however much in secret they may rebel, grow dumb in thy presence."

> The consciousness of duty done
> Is sweet as love when first 't is won.

There is no endowment which is not educable. Such power lies latent in every soul, that it is possible to bring health out of disease, strength out of weakness, knowledge out of ignorance, wisdom out of folly, and beauty out of ugliness. From the feeble elements of infant life, we can form sages, saints, and heroes. Order, punctuality, truthfulness, modesty, politeness, honesty, self-control, frugality, honor, and industry are the result of habits more than of endowment; and when right life prevails in the home and the school, children readily acquire the qualities which go to the making of character. What is virtue but a habit of right thinking and right doing? He who knows how to teach will find learners; he who knows how to learn will find teachers. "Girls," says Richter, "should be educated like the priestesses of antiquity, only in holy places; and they should not be permitted to hear, much less to see, aught that is rude, immoral, or violent." When we tell the young that education will bring them riches and honors, our words differ little from those of Satan, offering the Saviour cities and kingdoms, if he would adore him. Though thou feel that praise is sweet, and censure hard to bear, yet if praise or blame influence thy work, it is not great. Each soul is an original. Precisely such an one as thou or I has not lived from the beginning of time, nor shall, to its end. Let each one do his work, for to no other has God given it to do. " The quarters of an hour," said Napoleon, "decide the issue of battle." The quarters of an hour make the difference in the lives of men. It is a small matter if the Pope or the President be thy friend; but it is all important that thou be the friend of truth and justice.

Why read a long story to learn a truth which an aphorism will teach thee? A proverb is a true word. This is so; though, like all proverbs, it must be taken largely and not in a captious spirit. The proverb teaches wisdom, not criticism. It becomes old; but he who sees himself reflected therein renews his youth. Let him who would know a people study their proverbs. In them he finds their customs, habits, and occupations; their ways of feeling and seeing; their principles, experiences, and judgments; their aims and ends; their views of life and of the relative values of things. In them the common sense utters itself in simple words, without afterthought or disguise. They are a treasure-house of impersonal wisdom, which has grown with the life and language of the people, and is as permanent as they. They may be accredited to Solomon, or Homer, or Shakspere, or Goethe, but they belong to the race from which the man of genius has sprung.

If we can but persuade the young that education can be got, and that it is valuable, — of quite inestimable value, — half our work is done. Is it the fault of human nature, or is it that of teachers, that we have all crept like snails to school, and come away with nimble feet and glad hearts? Implant in the mind of the child the love of truth, the love of work and obedience. Herbert Spencer says that they who hope to engender better feelings by schooling the mental faculties are irrational. It would be as wise to attempt to teach geometry by giving lessons in Latin. But this is not a true view; for it is plain that thought influences feeling as feeling influences will. Self-respect is the basis of every virtue; and the best work the teacher can do is to nourish and strengthen self-respect. He who steals one's good name is but a petty thief; he who destroys self-respect is a murderer. If thou hast self-reverence, thou wilt put far away uncleanness of soul and body, insincerity, lying, and dishonesty. The test of a school is what it does for its inferior students, — the dull, the listless, and the unresponsive; for students of exceptional powers will educate themselves, unless they are put in the hands of mind-smotherers and heart-deadeners. The business of the teacher and that of the lecturer are diverse. The one seeks to get at and draw forth mind; the other, to elucidate and commend his subject. " Hence, " as Thring says, " a large audience stimulates the lecturer, but a large class overwhelms the teacher with despair; for he should treat each pupil as an individual and not as a member of a class." To listen, and to listen without impatience, to hear again and again the same objections, doubts, and grievances, confirms one's authority.

Nothing but faith in the power of sympathy and love can make the teacher an educator. The more easy his progress is made, the more readily will the child be brought to understand the use and necessity of labor. The more pleasant his work becomes, the more and higher work will he do. Let the educator devote himself wholly to forming wise and good men; for wise and good men are also true lovers of God and their country.

"One true thought," says Laurie, "take it whence you will, once fairly rooted in the mind of a boy, will do more for him, whether he is to be a shoemaker or a statesman, than grammar or calculus or the syllogism will do." There is an essential distinction between the elementary and the higher schools. In the elementary the pupils are trained to habits of work; in the higher, they are educated to self-activity, made capable of helping themselves, and of fulfilling whatever task may be assigned to them. It requires a certain maturity of mind to enable us to perceive that we do not necessarily know that of which we make constant use. Hence the grammar of the mother-tongue is apt to be an unprofitable study for children. It seems probable, indeed, that no one ever acquires a mastery of his own language except through the study of one that is foreign; and for this purpose none have such value as the Greek and the Latin. The educational worth of the Latin, for us at least, is greater than that of the Greek; for not only is our English speech largely of Latin origin, but our civilization, our religion, our laws and government, are, to a great extent, derived from Rome. The Greek, however, both as a language and a literature, is superior to the Latin. The breath which blows through the Greek classics exhilarates like mountain air; it brings fresh thoughts and glad anticipations; it is alive with the spirit of freedom and the glow of beauty. There the winged words, which fan the imaginations of millions, spring from the mind of genius as naturally as buds open in the air of spring. When I recall my early years in college, I find that the books of those in the higher classes made a mysterious impression on me, as though I felt that in them lay the secret and promise of richer life. I did not envy the athletes, but the youths of intellect and industry seemed to me to have set sail for the isles of the Blest. And now, as it all comes back to me, I know by reason as then I knew by instinct, how infinitely mind excels muscle.

He knows not what he yet may do,
Who works and to high aims keeps true.

A fresh and active spirit in the teacher and in the pupil is an indispensable requisite for the best school-work. But nothing is so rare; for the teacher is made heavy by the monotony and drudgery of his task, and the dull teacher makes the pupil dull. Is there no remedy? None, except the employment of thoroughly educated minds, who with profound faith in education, derived from experience of its efficacy in themselves, have in their own thoughts an inexhaustible source of sympathy and enthusiasm. The ideal position for the teacher is that of the master, who, like Plato and Aristotle, — like the Saviour himself, — is surrounded and followed by his disciples. But to hold this position, one must have a great mind or a great character. The more we trust to plans, systems, methods, apparatuses, and subject-matters of education, the more feeble and faulty will be the education which we give.

> " As day by day I older grow
> A deeper longing springs to know,
> Yet would I learn but from the brave."

" For this, I think," says Plato, " will be conceded to me, that only the brave or virtuous man can be a teacher."

CHAPTER III.

THOUGHTS AND THEORIES.

To noble minds fair words of truth
Are ever welcome and most sooth.

THE man of genius is not so much one who brings forth from his inner life new and profound thoughts, as one who, with immense power of receptivity, lays hold on the myriad impressions and utterances, which all may receive and hear, melts them in the divine fire, and moulds them into forms of truth and beauty. He is a painter, a sculptor, an architect, who works with the materials which all may have, but which he alone can transform into symbols of the infinite and all-perfect. The tales from which Shakspere drew Hamlet, Othello, Macbeth, and King Lear were crude stories. The orator produces his highest effect, when inspired by a casual remark, or an incident which another would not have stopped to consider. The soughing of the winds, the sobbing of the sea, the mutterings of the coming storm, the crackling of the fire, which all may hear, suggest celestial harmonies to him only who is born with a soul musically creative. When we perceive what appears to us to be good or beautiful, we unite it, by an act of the will, with ourselves; thus forming a whole, of which we and the object of our love are the parts. The higher the being to which we join our own, and the more complete the union, the greater our strength and joy. Will rather than intellect is the ultimate principle of human life, and the highest function of will is love. " The sovereign good for each one," says Descartes, " consists in the firm will to do right, and in the consent which such will produces ; for there is no other good which seems to be so great or so entirely in the power of every one." Strive to help others, for to be of service to none is to be nobody. The vanity of things is the correlative of man's feebleness of thought. All seems unsubstantial because we can know only modes of being, but can never comprehend being itself. Forced to live in a world of images and sensations, we weary of the idle spectacle and of the futile attempts to still appetites with shadows.

The sciences are nothing else than the mind of man insinuating itself into the intricacies of nature, and reducing all things to its own simplicity. The only kind of existence which it is possible for us to conceive, is existence in and for conscious beings. Materialism, therefore, has no meaning. The incomprehensibility of the divine nature is a principle of religion as of philosophy; and to this extent all reasonable men are agnostics. Ideas belong to a higher world than facts; they are facts interfused with thought, transformed by spirit, and floating in the abysmal being of God. He who has made himself at home in the world of ideas cannot envy mere doers, whether they be men of blood or men of gold. The passions of the mind have more vitality than those of the heart; they remain longer alive and active. If we could reason on all subjects with the care and impartiality with which a mathematician works out a problem, there would be hope that we might free ourselves from error. But even in adding up our bank accounts, we find it difficult not to make our credits too large, our debits too small.

To increase the power of the mind of man is a thing altogether higher than to add to the sum of his knowledge. The one belongs to God or to genius; the other, any plodder may hope to do. Plato and Aristotle were caught up centuries ago into the Invisible; but the ideas by which they lived are as present to us as the oceans and the stars. Tell me not of the labor thy work has cost thee. If it is well done it will appear to have been done with ease ; and, in praising thy industry, thou takest from the pleasure thy performance should give. In the midst of general mediocrity, a genuine talent escapes notice, or attracts the attention of but a few; and even they will hardly appreciate its full significance. Philosophy, poetry, and religion remain true and sacred for all noble souls, in spite of the senseless reign of matter. For them facts cannot annul ideas. " For the creators of thought," says De Vigny, " the application of ideas to things is but a loss of time." The multitude take things as they find them, being unable or unwilling to sift the materials, which are the occasions of their joys and sorrows, through the fine sieve of thought. Hence the speculations of philosophic minds have no interest for them. To attempt to explain the problem of the asymptote to one who is ignorant of mathematics, would be absurd; but not less so than to expect the multitude to understand the highest intellectual, moral, and æsthetic truth. New discoveries and scientific theories startle the world for a time, and lead to much discussion; and then, having become assimilated to the mass of our mental possessions, life flows on much the same as it had always run. The Copernican Astronomy, Geology, and Evolution, which have accustomed us to the infinite in space and time, have ceased to impress; and they leave us still fixed to a little spot of earth, where we live but a day, and die as our fathers died, — believing in God, and trusting to Him to save us from perishing utterly.

It depends on ourselves whether we believe that all is a lie, or that truth is the infinite reality, the ultimate nature and essence of whatever is. He who feels that his own life is not utterly empty and meaningless, will not accept a philosophy of despair. To become mechanical is to fall from the power of life, back to the fatal sway of matter. Keep, therefore, thy spirit free and fluid. Practical natures are quick to mock at those they call dreamers, because they are unable to realize to what an extent the world of all of us is a thing of the mind, a flower of the fancy. Children live in dreamland, the young in the imagination; and in maturity and old age we dwell in conventional habitations which the social environment and our own efforts have constructed. Are not time and space the web and woof of our lives; and what are they but the setting of the mind? the ideal is our most real and true home. When we look habitually into the heart of things, the struggles and contentions of which we are witnesses seem idle as the disputes of children, that are forgotten as soon as the noise

dies away. The solitudes into which thought
drives its votaries, seem, at times, to be deserts
where the soul grows afraid of its proper world,
and longs for the power to relish the things
which make the unthinking laugh and cry. We
are all bedded on the lap of our great mother-
earth; and it is there only that we rest and
sleep as children rest and sleep. The facile
pleasures are so much more natural to man
than those which are born of the exercise of
his noblest endowments, that even a genius is
rarely able to resist the attraction of his animal instincts; for genius, like all that is high
within us, is enrooted in the sensuous nature,
and can flourish only in this soil, which nevertheless is rank, and when left to itself produces
but what is coarse, from even the finest seed.
To be interesting to the crowd, one must have
a touch of vulgarity. A philosopher is made
known, not by the profound truth he reveals,
but by the bearing which his teaching is sup-
posed to have on politics and popular religion,
on social and commercial life. Intellectual con-
querors are not accompanied by armies in glittering array, by the blare of trumpets and the
shoutings of mobs; but their triumphal march
proceeds and is acclaimed by the best, from
people to people, and from age to age, while
the war captains and politicians, with their cam-

paigns and noise of battle, die away in an echo.
If thou take more pleasure in seeing thy prejudices overcome by truth than in finding arguments to confirm thee in them, thy studies
shall cheer and lead thee to fairer worlds.
Cremonini, hearing that Galileo had discovered
the moons of Jupiter, refused to turn his tele-
scope to the planet, lest he should find that
Aristotle had been wrong. The world is full
of Cremoninis. The most godlike soul who
ever breathed earthly air was not surrounded
by diviner things than you or I. It was himself that made him great, and not the world
about him.

> " The fault, dear Brutus, is not in our stars,
>   But in ourselves, that we are underlings."

Only weak natures consent to dwell among
tombstones and the losses of which they are
the symbol; the strong drink wisdom and
courage from the cup of sorrow, and move
onward toward light and life. He who can
coin his worst disappointments into apothegms
passes through troubles and trials with a light
heart. The wise are indulgent, for they know
that men are weak rather than perverse. Their
indignation at the sight of evil is tempered by
the thought that the wicked are self-tormentors.
They are modest too, and are persuaded that

7

God makes the world, not they. The resplen-
dent dome of life, lifting itself into the heavens
and shooting its rays into infinities, rests on the
foundation of appetite and sexual desire. The
noblest mind has slept as a microscopic germ
within an intestine. The secret of what gives
the purest joy seems to lie open; but unless the
heavenly powers assist, we shall never find the
hidden spring which makes it ours. Who can
explain what it is in a man's conversation or
style that awakens interest and gives pleasure?
Why do we love a spring morning or a beautiful face, or the songs of birds, re-echoing from
bough to bough? Shall we pluck a rose, and
tear it leaf from leaf, to discover why it thrills
us with delight? Wherever human life is
whole, men believe that they are partakers
of the divine nature, and belong to an order
of things which is infinite and eternal. In this
faith they strive nobly; and, if failure or dis-
aster overtake them, they still hold that life is
good. Disillusions bring into view fairer and
wider prospects for those who have the courage
to look steadfastly. God made man to his own
image, and man is always striving to make the
world to his own likeness. You cannot content him with less than a universe, in which,
as in a mirror, he may see but the image of
himself. Genius is most disappointing when

its inspiration is most pure. We feel that now
the veil shall be lifted, the light that never yet
was seen appear; we wipe the tears from our
eyes, and behold but the common day. Even
if everything had been said, it would be necessary to repeat it, and in other words. What
the best minds see to be no longer tenable, will
little by little lose its hold on the multitude
also. The provokers of ideas have greater and
more enduring power than the stirrers of passion. Ideas are the highest which life's current
bears. Love is more satisfying, but it needs
the support of ideas. Great thoughts are so
rare that one is enough to make its author
famous. Be brave, cheerful, and industrious,
and good things will cluster around thee like
bees about flowers. Happy are they who begin life in an atmosphere which inspires confidence and serenity. Whatever troubles come
later, they will hardly lose faith in themselves
and the goodness of living. What we admire
is precious to us. Learn to admire, and thou
shalt be richer than kings. Who pleases is
master; who ceases to please, nobody.

It is futile to strive to isolate ourselves, for
we are not separate but only appear to be so.
The roots which nourish our life shoot out in
every direction, the tap root striking down into
the Absolute and Eternal. Hence springs the

yearning for immortality, the longing to sur-
vive as an influence, whether our thought be
of a few or of mankind. They who hate us do
us less despite than they who forget us. It is
not the world in which it was possible for thee
to live, but the world in which thou hast actu-
ally made thyself a home, which constitutes thy
significance and proves thy worth. They who
cannot understand our highest thoughts or sym-
pathize with our divinest moods are strangers,
though they be our brothers and sisters; for
we live in that which is best and strongest in
us, and it is there that we are truly ourselves.
The craving for eternal love is less sensibly felt·
by a few, at least, than the craving for absolute
truth. Their hearts are near breaking, not because they fear they shall not live and love forever, but because they fear they shall never
truly know. He who is able for his work does
it with a brave and cheerful heart. The noise
of his tools sounds in his ears like a song. Be
strong and wise, and thou shalt not lack for
followers and helpers.

"A man who will make no effort for himself," says Demosthenes, "need not apply for
aid to his friends and much less to the gods."
A great thought, whatever the form in which it
is uttered, is great, as a great soul, whatever its
body, is great; but noble thoughts will find fit·

ting expression. "By a long habit of writing,"
says Goldsmith, "one acquires a greatness of
thinking and a mastery of manner which mere
holiday writers, with ten times the genius, may
vainly attempt to equal." There is magic in
the pen. Its touch is magnetic, and sets the
spirit at work. It rouses from lethargy, and
brings us back to the world of truth and beauty.
It is hardly grasped when thought begins to
flow. · Though our minds seem dry and barren
as the rocks, the pen will cause living waters to
spring from them; and along the channels they
take, flowers will bloom and birds will sing.

The pen is a divining rod which shows where
lie the hidden veins; it is a revealer who makes
us known to ourselves; it is a wonder-worker
who, from evanescent moods and flashes of
light, weaves for truth an enduring vesture,
wherein it may draw near to the homes and
hearts of men, and receive welcome, like a
visitant from God. The orator requires fit
audience and the urgency of a great occasion;
but the writer is happiest when he thinks not
of the reader, and he needs no other occasion
than that which true thoughts bring. He utters
himself that he may find and know himself, and
his reward is sufficient though no eye but his
own ever rest upon his page.

Write the best thou knowest, thy holiest faith,

without a thought of what impression it shall make, but simply as a testimony to thyself and to truth. To lose consciousness of one's self in the presence of what is divine — to be so carried away by the vision of truth that self sinks out of sight — is to be in the mood for the exercise of creative intellectual power. To say well that with which all are familiar has no great merit; the test of a writer's skill is his ability to give correct and adequate expression to what is original and profound. However vital the truth, if there is a flaw in the expression, some one will stamp it more authentically and make it his own. The foolish write of what they believe to be false; the wise tell the truth they know.

Even in the best writers there is much that is inferior in thought and style, as in the fairest landscape there is much that is commonplace. In Dante as in Milton, in Plato as in Shakspere, there are wastes where we find no refreshment; there are heavinesses which we feel to be burdens; there are things uninteresting in themselves about which no breath of inspiration is blown; but on the heights to which they bear us again and again, all this is forgotten or pardoned.

When there is a vivid consciousness of the truth which we wish to utter, the right expression is not difficult to find. Truths which we have pondered and loved for a long time, seem little by little to transfuse themselves into the substance of our souls, and when we utter them there is a vital quality in our words. It is this intimate acquaintance with truth which gives proportion, adequacy, and naturalness to style. Learn to love ideas for themselves; and do not think, the instant a truth dawns on thee, of devising a new scheme for reforming the world. Is it not a gain that fresh ideas circulate, and that the minds of even a few are stimulated to a disinterested self-activity?

"To accustom mankind," says Joubert, "to pleasures which depend neither upon the bodily appetites nor upon money, by giving them a taste for the things of the mind, seems to me the one proper fruit which nature has meant our literary productions should bear." They who have a sort of rule of thumb whereby they determine the value of the products of the mind, have no interest for us; for we feel, without entering further into their views, that life is infinitely deeper, richer, and wider than they are able to conceive. They are like one who, standing beneath the starlit vault, should point out and name the constellations, and would have us believe that he has thereby opened to our gaze the abysmal depths of the heavens.

Names and formulas are but the shell; and the soul craves for the inner heart of truth. Commentators and critics are like cicerones who take travellers to see the masterpieces of the great artists. Their learned chatter hinders the impression which the works themselves should make. The author's intentions are of importance to himself, but not to the world which judges him by his work. The masters of style themselves are seldom fully aware of its worth and importance. Half the errors and controversies which fill the world with confusion would cease to exist if men spoke and wrote with clearness and accuracy. Truth rightly expressed is its own evidence; and beauty of style is the glow which truth irradiates. Formal and mechanical minds have been the cause of half our woe and misery. Believe, hope, love, and work, welcoming each day as an opportunity given thee by God to grow like unto Him, who is truth, power, goodness, and beauty. Compare thyself often with thy idea of human perfection, and it will be easy for thee to keep thyself modest and humble. If diffidence come over thee, and thou doubt whether thou shalt ever be able to do a noble deed or utter a memorable word, call to mind the example of those who have triumphed over greater obstacles than thou hast to surmount. Words do not reveal the best, which can be made plain only by action. "Single thoughts," says Diesterweg, " read or heard in the course of conversation, have been of more weight with me than hourlong teaching." If thou wouldst educate thyself, follow the advice of St. Paul: "Prove all things, hold fast to that which is good." We know only what forms an organic union with our minds, and thus becomes part of ourselves. Be suspicious of thy sincerity when thou art the advocate of that upon which thy livelihood depends. If thou hast done aught of good, forget it. Thy business is not with what is done, but with what remains to do.

Insist not upon the truth thou knowest. Utter it as best thou art able, and leave it like seed-corn till the glow of minds and hearts shall call it forth into the light of day. Never believe that thou hast done thy best; and turn, therefore, from praise which is due only to those who have done their best. Unless thy view of truth is profound, thou shalt not feel secure except in shallow places. Life is so complex and our sight so feeble, that even the wisest play but a game of chance. Good fortune is good sense; but no forethought can save from great calamities. Put, then, thy trust in the Eternal, in whom all things are reconciled. Stop not to think what thou mightest have done, but keep thyself busy doing what it is right to do. Let each moment, as it falls from Eternity, whether it find thee sick or well, happy or miserable, bear thee nearer to wisdom and goodness, even as it bears thee nearer to death. Let nothing go to waste, nor time nor money, nor aught of which time and money are the equivalents. The day in which we have learned nothing is lost. Think and speak of what thou lovest, and dwell little on what is distasteful to thee. The habit of contemplating truth, goodness, and beauty in the spirit of a disinterested curiosity is fatal. They are of the essence of our being, they are our life; and we must love them or we become the enemies of our own souls. Passive acquiescence in opinions and beliefs has no efficacy; it impels neither to thought nor action, but rather dulls the mind and weakens the will. The value of our faith is measured by the power with which we react upon it. Intellectual and moral freedom is won by long and hard battles with the sensual nature which holds young souls captive. In the struggle conscience emerges, and the real man begins to be. Strive in the light of the ideal of humanity to make thyself a man, without the shadow of a doubt that thou canst thereby lose aught of good or best which life can give.

Once we have found the work which we were born to do, the only thing we seem to lack is time. They are wise who lead a laborious and hidden life, nourished by the love of one or two, and devoted to the search for truth and the practice of good. It is to little purpose that we are good mechanics or good rulers, if we ourselves are starved and warped. He who has no fear of death hardly thinks of it at all. If thou needest recognition, content thyself with life in a narrow sphere; but, if thou wouldst influence many, be prepared to find thyself misunderstood and abused. Strive ceaselessly to form in thyself a brave and contented spirit, and to give strength and happiness to those who come under thy influence. Work is the only distraction which can make us forget the miseries of life. ʻWhoever has lived in the company of the truly great is made interesting. Desire influence over others only for their own and the general good. No human being is as wise or good or strong or fair or happy as I would have him be. If it were better with all others, it would be better with me. Fame is not happiness; but delight in doing the things which win fame is happiness. To be strong one should live much alone and belong to no party. If the course of things disturb thee, consider that the end for which the world exists

could not be thwarted even by a conspiracy
of the whole race.

To be religious we must serve God, not with
one faculty, but with all, which we must develop
and cultivate on every side. Whatever palaces
we build, if we ourselves are vulgar and ignorant, we live in the midst of poverty and squalor.
If thou must now lack what once gave thee joy,
be thankful that for a time it was thine. · Take
sickness as a task God sets thee, which thou
must get through with as best thou mayst; and
thou shalt find that courage and good sense will
help thee to recover from thy illness. Many
are sick because they have not the heart to be
well. In each individual there lies hidden a
better man than the one whom daily life brings
to the surface. To discover and rouse this
higher self to activity is the educator's aim, as
it is that of the apostle. They who lead the
life of thought and contemplation, know the
best which can fall to the lot of man on earth.
If thou wouldst not feel the pain of want, content thyself with little; find pleasure, like Socrates, in thinking how many things the world
is full of which thou dost not need. We may
learn to accept irreparable losses with a mild
sadness which becomes a solace and a blessing.
In the midst of a world which is forever passing away, cleave with all thy might to the

Eternal, to whom thou art akin; for else the
evanescence of things would not sadden thee.
Fortunate is he who need ask nothing of men,
except the pleasure which their happiness
gives him. Boast not of thyself or thy possessions; for to do so is not only vulgar, but a
sign of the folly which goes before a fall. If
thy descent is high, let it be shown by thy
deeds, not by thy words. God sees whole
worlds perish, and is not disturbed. Hold fast
to Him, and thou shalt not lose thy composure.
The mass of events pass before us like a spectacle, in which it is not possible to take more
than a momentary interest. Let not this
theatrical world distract thee from thy proper
good. In a hundred years the human race
renews itself three times: in thirty-three years,
fifteen hundred millions are born and die; each
year, some forty millions. Three times within
a century the whole race comes upon the stage,
plays its part, amid laughter and tears, then
falls asleep in darkness and vanishes utterly.
Receive good and bad fortune with a like
welcome, since thou canst not know which
may better help thy progress in wisdom and
virtue. The pleasures we refuse to take will
return to us in higher and more enduring
form. God gives us peace as He gives us
wisdom, only when we ourselves have fought

the battles and won the victories which make
them ours.

> Who strives with earnest will has half attained,
> For in the striving richer life is gained.

Happy days vanish and leave scarce a trace
behind; but sad days go away too, and if we
have known how to use them, they leave us
stronger and wiser. If thy thought and love
make thy happiness, thou canst not lose it
while thou remainest thyself. We may not
rest in the enjoyment of what our labors have
achieved, but must make it the means to the at-
tainment of yet higher good. They who are
busy stilling their appetites, that is, deadening
their pain, have no time to be happy. God
Himself cannot make it possible that men shall
find happiness except in the fulfilment of duty
and in love. All things come and go, rise into
view and vanish, and man cannot stay their
course. Accept the fact without complaint, and
float thy little day upon the ceaseless stream,
trusting that, when life's bubble shall burst, God
will receive thee into more enduring worlds.
Though thou standest on the brink of the grave,
hope thou mayst yet do some good deed before
death comes. To rest in anything which makes
us happy, though it be the love of wife and
children, of home and friends, leads to a soft

and indolent temper. In the love of God we
cannot rest, for the love of God is effort and
infinite desire. It is the love of the best which
can never be wholly ours. He who lives in his
thoughts and in the emotions which they
awaken, needs little else for his entertainment;
and as he needs little for himself he is the more
able to be of help to others. They alone know
the sweetness and worth of virtue, in whom the
combat has died away into habits of right doing.
They are like heroes whose victories have made
men free, and who now sit at home in peace,
surrounded by those they love. Thy influence
over the few whom thou knowest can be but
slight; and over the many, if it exist at all, it
is necessarily insignificant. Trouble not thyself, then, about what thou canst not change,
but rise into the calm region of truth, where
what is known and loved is forever fair and
good; and in this way, perchance, better than
in another, thou mayst be of help to thy fellows.
Truth is so divinely sweet that they who have
entered the inner sanctuary of knowledge lead
a blessed life, though they are outcast from the
world or in prison. Our happiness, indeed, like
our unhappiness, is largely illusion; there being
seldom any necessary connection between our
joys or sorrows and the things to which we at-
tribute them. Where man feels impotent to

react against nature or the course of things, he settles into some kind of fatalism. In the tropics this temper prevails; and in Europe and with us, those who are persuaded that there is nothing but nature, feel that they are borne helplessly on the boundless stream of tendency.

"The era of universal mediocrity is beginning," says Amiel; "everything is becoming less gross, but more vulgar. The day of great men is passing away; society is settling on a monotonous plain where there are no undulations. The statistician will remark a general progress, the moralist a general decline, — progress of things, decline of souls." Let not thoughts like these disturb thee; but know that God is in His world, appealing to men as of old to rise heavenward. Pessimism is a temper, not a philosophy. As a system of thought it is not deserving of serious consideration.

The universe is at once the worst and the best, for there is no other; and the brave and healthy find it a good enough world for those who live for truth and love; but a cowardly and despairing spirit would make a hell of heaven. We rebel against want, but it is our great teacher. The desert reveals the worth of water; sickness, that of health; age, that of youth. He who has never eaten his bread with tears, the poet

says, knows not the heavenly powers; and they
who have all they desire are not or soon shall
cease to be men. That all is vanity none of
us genuinely believe; and if we so believed we
should be neither Christian nor sensible. God
is not vanity, nor is the universe which is athrill
with God. A well trained sophist will prove
any thing from anything, and convert whatever
words and events to his whim; but the serious
shrink from his methods as being nothing else
than a profanation of reason. Syllogisms are
crutches for crippled minds. Whatever I read
in praise of childhood, youth, manhood, or old
age, I say to myself: The period of life which
is now mine is the most precious, and, if I but
make right use of it, it will give me the best.

> Here or nowhere, now or never,
> Let each one strive with best endeavor.

"Terse sentences," says Cicero, "have great
weight as aids to a happy life."

Let us live and let live in the things of the
mind as in other things. We may believe and
yet be unable to prove our faith; may doubt the
validity of all the arguments which have been
advanced in its support. What is false is not
less so because a thousand years ago it was
believed to be true; nor is what is true less so
because then it was believed to be false. Who-

ever acts, whoever utters honest thought, runs the risk of doing harm; but not to act and not to utter honest thought is not to be a man. The measure of a man's worth is the industry and perseverance with which he seeks truth, speculative and practical. He who sweeps the altar steps performs divine service, if he work in the right spirit. Health and the will to work carry us far. Do thy best, and be glad that many do their best. Love thy country, but so as not to hinder the larger love thou owest all thy kind. Good deeds and high thoughts go forth to make us friends whom we shall never know. Speak of thy joys; leave thy sorrows, like thy dead, in their graves. Soft words soothe harsh tempers as raindrops calm angry waves. Deeds are the substance of history; but words, which make literature, are also deeds.

While the national life continues to develop, the love of science, literature, and art continues to increase; religion continues to be nourished by self-renewing faith, and all the higher interests prosper; but when the nation's life begins to decay, individuals sicken and lose heart, and all that strengthens and gladdens the soul tends toward extinction. We may hold before the eyes of youth, as incentives to industry, prospects of honor and wealth; but the only worthy result of study is the wisdom, courage, and fidelity with which it informs the mind and conscience. When genius makes use of its divine power to render sin alluring and to throw a glamour around vice, it is as though a hero should become a pimp or a beautiful woman a harlot. They who set truth in a new light render service scarcely less important than they who discover new truth, which after all can hardly be more than a new phase of truth. If thy one object is truth, what matter whether thou find it with thy friends or thy foes? If thou hearest it from the lips of a convict, it is sacred as though it had been spoken by the holiest of men. Though worlds be shattered, let truth be sought and found, be loved and proclaimed. It is the life of the mind, and to hinder its pursuit is a crime against humanity. Where thou art unable to speak truth in its purity, attempt not to express it at all.

> That truth is fair all gladly do confess,
> But naked? Shame! it must have on a dress.

Sow the seed of the harvest thou hopest to reap in the soil of thine own language and country. If it strike not root there, it will not anywhere. Be true to those who love thee and whose love thou hast accepted, though it cost thee the good-will of all others, though it cost thee thy life. Help without sympathy is mockery, — it is the pity which is harder to bear than pain. We need little; but we must have liberty to strive for all, since we are born for God and the Universe. The aureole which encircles truth sheds a purer light than the approving smile of millions. It dims the splendor of the crowns of kings and of the jewels which sparkle on the milk-white breast of beauty. Sunlight diffuses itself through boundless space ; and it is fairest when it is reflected from the noblest objects, — from planets and moons and the azure vault of heaven, from evening and morning skies, from limpid streams and snowy peaks. So truth pervades the Universe, and it is most beautiful when its mirror is the noblest mind. Though ancient as the stars, it is born again in the soul of genius, and issues thence, clothed in new glory, to refresh and gladden the hearts of men. We may learn to be happy as we may learn whatever else is desirable. We are, in fact, happy when we are busy providing for ourselves and others what is good and useful; and though the fruit of our toil be small, the labor itself makes the waters of life fresh and pleasant. The wider and higher the world thou consciously livest in, the greater thy opportunities to enrich and purify thy life. If thou art tempted to envy or hate any one, think of the sufferings, sorrows, and disappointments which he has had to bear, of those which surely must still befall him, and thy heart shall be softened. In presence of what is inevitable or irremediable, resignation is not difficult. If we lose a hand or an eye, we make shift without it. Each moment brings death nearer; but since there is no escape, we are not greatly troubled. We are more disturbed by a calamity which threatens than by one which has befallen us. Necessity teaches us to bear that of which the thought is intolerable. However much we be afraid to die, when the inexorable messenger presents himself, he shall seem less terrible than we apprehend. From the most solemn subjects jests and witticisms rise like vapors from deep seas. They are suggested by life and death, by love and religion, by friendship and marriage. They serve as a relief from thoughts which lie too deep for tears. One who strives to bring about changes in the world around him may easily be thwarted; but he who labors with himself to improve his own mind and heart has the freedom of the Universe, the liberty of the children of God, and cannot be impeded. The best educate and make themselves. Life and the great masters and obstinate labor are their teachers.

" Our demagogues," says Schopenhauer, "would have us believe that, if governments did their duty, the kingdom of heaven would appear; to wit, that all men would be able, without difficulty, to stuff themselves with food and drink, to cohabit and dissolve into dust, — for this is what they mean when they talk of the progress of mankind." Unless thou turn from dreams of salvation through numbers and majorities, and give thy whole thought to truth and goodness, thou shalt make no progress nor become able to render divine help. Thou must somehow lay hold on the Eternal, or else thy soul, having no deep root, will wither and be lost. If thou feelest that thou hast done little good, there is at least much evil which thou hast not done. The saint finds blessedness in losing himself that he may find himself in God; no longer now a petty egoist, but part of the divine life and universal harmony. In this spirit the worthiest work. Not to weave a wreath about a name, but to get at the inner heart of truth and goodness, a noble man lives and strives. When, therefore, we meet with one who would link his name with whatever may feed his vanity, we sadly smile, as when we hear the old, whose minds have grown feeble, speak words which show that they have lost their hold on the real world and are wandering amid shadowy things. The infinite Power from whom the universal fact proceeds is now as it has been from the beginning; and if ever anywhere souls have been able to draw thence faith, hope, and love, thou mayst here and now. The ideas from which the thoughts and deeds of great hearts spring are few and simple. Any one may understand them; but in the great heart they are not mere ideas, but substance and life. The right temper makes the worst situation tolerable; but no situation can redeem the craven from misery. Pericles is as serene in the midst of the pest, himself pest-stricken, as when he watches the temples of the Acropolis rise in celestial splendor against the sky of Attica. The beauty which we do not own, which is associated with no sordid interests, has the greatest charm. The stars and the moon, the sunset and the dawn, the leafy hills and the snowy peaks, the wild-flowers and the songs of wild birds, of the lark in the blue heavens and of the nightingale, up-perched amid cool and bunched leaves, young girls who are heartwhole and fancy free, — are all the fairer, because they are the possession of no man, but belong to worlds where mine and thine — those frigid words — are unknown.

The alchemists sought what cannot be found, — the secret of converting baser metals into gold; but to their labors we owe our chemistry, which has given us a world of precious things that mountains of gold could not have provided. If thou seekest pleasure or money or fame, and findest in the end that thou hast gotten only insight and wisdom, be thankful. Expect little of life, and the good it brings will be doubly blessed. No one renounces his faith for honor or gold. He may seem to do so, but he only seems. If thy love of thy possessions be not excessive, thou shalt not fear those who have power to deprive thee of them. Profound convictions are traditional, and they who have relaxed their hold on the past have but feeble spiritual life. From a base soul nothing divine can spring. The very virtues of servile natures are faults. Their obedience is cowardice; their love, selfishness; their faith, a calculation; their chastity, an accident; their humility, human respect. God made thee free, Christ has clothed thee with a higher liberty; and wilt thou still bear the heart of a slave, or believe that He who made thee would have thee crawl and cringe, and not assert thy immortal self and kinship with Him? Civilization, like religion, is the work of an apostolate, which appeals to man's faith, hope, and love, to his need of truth and beauty, to his yearning for life in God and in humanity. Schopenhauer thinks that the necessity of laws to punish crime argues the impotence of religious faith. But civilization has sprung from religious faith and has sought in it the sanction of its moral and legal code. Hence we may say that religion makes the laws by which crime is punished; while criminals themselves are found chiefly among those who have no religion.

Truth is the end of science; beauty, of art; love, of religion: and truth, beauty, and love are a trinity. Take care first of thy moral, then of thy physical, and lastly of thy intellectual health. There are words whose very sound moves and exalts the soul, — magnanimity, love, energy, freedom, truth. To speak them is to feel that we are God's men. It is an advantage to belong to the minority. We thus escape the baseness of those who run with the crowd, and are urged to show, in our own lives, that truth and virtue may lift a man to worlds where votes count for nothing. The majority have never been with the noblest souls; and, when the multitude have followed in the wake of divine minds, they have been drawn by the hope of material, not of spiritual good. The Saviour, whose heart throbbed with sympathy for the many, looked to the few to know and understand him. They whose spiritual nature lies dormant, while their appetites are alive and active, are animals; or they may be called fools, since they have no sense of man's proper good. He who interests me in any high or worthy thing does me better service than he who gives me great place or wealth. In speaking of the highest things a serious man may say that he does not know, but he may not imply that he does not care. If men care not for thee, it is not because they bear thee ill-will, but because thou hast failed to interest and help them; and whether thy failure come of lack of power in thyself or of lack of appreciation in them, accept the fact and continue to strive.

> Give me a work to do,
>   This is the richest gift;
> The heart no rest can woo
>   Unless work bring it shrift.

Living knowledge is that which we put to use, which remains with us as a source of light and strength. As a child stretches forth its hand to grasp everything, so let a man apply his mind to all that God has made. They are wise who are taught wisdom by the events of daily life. A watch counts the seconds, and so does a wise man. He dies richest from whom the greatest number inherit the fairest gifts. When we have attained the highest point of our spiritual growth, the knowledge and wisdom which we have gained serve chiefly to throw a purer and holier light on the dreams, hopes, and loves of our childhood. When a stick was for me a horse, grains of corn my flocks and herds, and a game of marbles as interesting as now the rivalries and struggles of men, — happy was I, having the divine power to make a world out of nothing.

> Like to a star,
> Without rest,
> Without haste,
> Let each one revolve
> 'Bout his God-given task.

He whose mind is uplit by great thoughts, which he follows with steadfast will, has an antidote for life's poisons. The sun is afire, the earth is awhirl, the atoms are athrill; souls are believing, hoping, loving; God lives. Why should I be troubled? Thou wilt not hurt me, O my God! or if Thou punish, Thou wilt do it at the behest of love, and because it is right.

Heat, light, electricity, — love, knowledge, genius. Once thou knowest what thou art born to do, wait not to be called, heed not when men forbid. That which it is always well to have, be the business what it may, is not so much an orator, a journalist, or a scholar, as a man of good sense and discernment, capable of judging rightly, and incapable of acting without prudence and courage. But where is the school in which the chief aim and effort is to form such men? Nature is wholly matter of fact, without any touch of sentiment; and she thrusts aside the foolish and incompetent as though they had no right to exist at all. There is no better test of truth than its helpfulness. It is joy, freedom, and power; it clothes life with higher meaning and impels it to diviner issues. But error is confusion and weakness. It keeps no promise, inspires no heroic moods, and leaves us, at the end, with a sense of the illusiveness of all things.

> All other things I do because I ought,
> But this, my soul, because I will and must.

The whole business of science is to discover what is and happens, and how it is and happens. Further than this it does not go. Why, then, should any soul alive wish to quarrel with science? He in whose words we find ever anew fresh sources of inspiration is a true master. Test thy thought by deeds, thy deeds by thought. We hear but what we understand and see but what we know. One's relations with the incompetent are always unsatisfactory. To lead a quiet, contented, and unpretentious existence is, I suppose, best for all, but certainly for those who would give themselves to a life of thought.

A genial humanity, kindly, cheerful, modest, open, and tolerant is what the Germans mean by their great word, " Gemüthlichkeit." It is a virtue we all need to cultivate. A wise man is slow to denounce one who, whatever his faults, has great qualities. Foolish, then, is he who vituperates a people which has played an important part in the history of the world. Abuse is vulgar, and vulgarity is largely ignorance. An undue opinion of one's own importance is a mark of an unbalanced mind. It needs but a little exaggeration to become one of the common forms of insanity. The good of life lies in the possibility it affords, to beings born ignorant, to bring themselves into conscious and sympathetic union with all that is true, good, and beautiful; and to make this possibility a reality is the task imposed by the heavenly powers on each one, as he enters the world. Let it be thy aim to unite the love of beauty with simplicity, intellectual culture with moral purpose, and ceaseless striving with a calm spirit.

In art God reveals Himself as beauty; in philosophy and science, as truth; in conduct and religion, as righteousness and love. Virtues are nourished by weaknesses and wants. Intelligence and moral strength are the results of our own efforts. and of those of our forefathers, to escape hunger, cold, disease, and dangers of a thousand kinds. Our maladies have not only given us insight into the structure of the body, and led to the discovery of means of prevention and cure; but they have taught us sympathy and all the delicate service of charity and love. The privation of what we desire has inspired the labors to which we owe the marvellous inventions that enable us almost to suppress distance and time. The conscious-ness of ignorance, which is most intense in the most powerful minds, has given the impulse to the studies from which our philosophy and science have sprung. The sense of the lack of beauty has spurred genius to its immortal creations. Hopeless loss has made us aware of the worth of resignation, courage, and mag-nanimity. Tyranny and injustice have brought home to us the value of freedom and law; and our sins and vices have made us understand our boundless need of the infinite mercy of God. Thus suffering and sorrow, which seem to be our enemies, are heavenly messengers sent to teach us how we may attain higher and purer life.

Our sympathy extends not to our fellow-men alone, but to all things, — to dogs and horses and birds; to the house we live in or where live those we love; to our city, our country; to hills and streams; to the pen we write with; to the chair we sit in; to the flowers and the stars and the trees; to sorrows, perhaps, which have been with us so long that they seem to have become part of ourselves; to caged animals; to criminals and outcasts; to viewless atoms; and to whatever else may help to bind the universe about the feet of God and around the heart of man. Let us not think meanly of matter, which is God's creature, — the expression of His will, and the witness of His power and wisdom.

Until the Copernican astronomy was established the revolution of the celestial bodies around the earth was as true as any other phenomenon. It fitted into the general order of nature and was part of its uniformity. Now it is no longer a fact but an illusion. This is but a feeble example of the transformation which the universe of material things undergoes in passing through the philosophic mind. Sensation first, then thought; and in the end, as in the beginning, faith.

Generous souls hide their good deeds as though they were evil. If all that the heart can desire were given us, the motive of action would cease to exist and life would lose its charm. They alone appreciate the masterpiece in whom its contemplation calls forth the mood in which the genius created his work. The genuinely good — the gentle, patient, loving, and helpful souls, who bear all and think no evil, who minister without a thought of self — have divine power. In their presence genius is obscured, and beauty bows in recognition of a higher and holier splendor of truth.

The scientific view does not impel to conduct. Physicians are apt to neglect their health; theologians are not pious; philosophers have little wisdom; and men of science them- selves are wanting in faith, the chief source of conduct. Whatever a sensible author writes is an Essay on Man. The mind, not the body, inspires the purest and most enduring love. It is difficult for the rich to know whether they are loved for themselves; and hence they easily become hard and distrustful. It profits nothing to dwell on wrongs suffered by our- selves or our ancestors, unless they remind us of the courage with which they were borne. The knowledge which leads us to contemn any- thing is not wisdom. A single mind has given here and there a new point of view to succeed- ing generations, and has thus compelled the thoughts and efforts of men into new channels. Or shall we not rather say, that an impulse from God, communicating itself through single minds, works these wonders? We no sooner give evidence of ability than we are appealed to, to speak, to write, to act; and this appeal is made when we are immature, and, like the immature, long for recognition, and find praise sweet. The result is that we are drawn into the world when we most need to live within ourselves, that we may learn to cherish the inner sources of power. We get applause or money, and soon grow blind to the ignominy of bartering the noblest gifts for emptiness or mere matter; and, as a consequence, we neither upbuild our being nor perform anything of enduring worth.

Persons alone are interesting; and when in a book an original personality is revealed, we inevitably yield to its charm. Physical, political, and social liberty is necessarily limited; and, when we attempt to overstep its bounds, we fall into folly or license. Let us be content if we have enough for health and the work we were born to do; and turn our thoughts to the inner world of truth and goodness, which is the birthplace and home of freedom. If thy endowments are rich they will require a long time to unfold themselves; and thou shalt easily acquire industry and patience, for thou shalt feel that the best in thee has not yet been brought into act. The decisive thing for each one is the intelligence and steadfastness with which he follows a life-aim, whether it be high or common. In striving still to hold what has lost meaning and the power to nourish life, we do harm to our spiritual nature, as the body suffers when what becomes effete within it is not eliminated. Words are to deeds as woman is to man. As the sound of cataracts is more distinctly heard at night, so the voice of conscience speaks in clearer accents from the midst of the gloom in which sorrow envelops us. God has so made us that we can find no genuine joy in destroying and denying, but only in creating and in affirming with new power the everlasting worth of truth and love. How many we see who have all earthly blessings, except the mind to use them right! How much importance even a great philosopher may attach to one of his thoughts we see in the instance of Hegel, who complains of Goethe for appropriating his explanation of the saying, that no man is a hero to his body servant; the reason being that the servile nature is incapable of understanding the heroic. As there is not a patriotic philosophy, science, or art, so there is not a patriotic religion, if it be true. "Trifles," said Michelangelo, "constitute perfection, and perfection is not a trifle." The gentle mind makes the gentleman.

> Religion shields with heaven-built wall
> The feebler sex, and thus safeguards us all.

If to-day I see that what I have held to be truth
is not truth, it follows that I have grown wiser;
and so I take fresh courage and sail for new
worlds. Life is full enough of disenchantments,
and the lessons they teach are not hard to learn.
Let us, then, if we would win the gratitude of
men, not discourage but inspire them with
brave and cheerful thoughts. There are things
in which to have great skill is a mark of inferior talent or judgment. When some one told
Antisthenes that Ismenias was an excellent
piper, he said: "It may be so; but he is a
poor sort of man, for else he would not be an
excellent piper." Since we cannot excel in
many things, let us apply ourselves to those
which are most deserving of the thought and
labor of immortal beings.

CHAPTER IV.

THOUGHTS AND THEORIES.

For me God made the light and air,
   Made also truth and love for me ;
They lie about me everywhere,
   And are my life and liberty.

FROM the sluggish and turbid stream of
current opinion, steer forth into the wide
and pacific ocean of truth, where thou mayst
hope to learn to know and love what God knows
and loves.

The noblest and purest sentiments and im-
pulses often lead to failure and unhappiness, as
though God would thus show us that the highest
and the best cannot be rewarded with material
gifts, but that there is a higher than happiness,
— the blessedness, namely, which is known
only to the sincerest and most loving souls. If,
on another planet, there are beings like ourselves, for them the earth is but a bright star
which glistens on the brow of evening or of
morning. Its barren mountains and deserts, its
tragedies of sin and sorrow and death, for them
have no existence. Only the light with its

glory and beauty penetrates the abysmal depths of space; and so they who look forth from eternity may see in God's universe but the light of love and truth.

If we approach nature in the right mood, she will not betray our trust. The hermit finds the bleak mountain full of peace and beauty. There silence is sweeter than music, the stars look down with a more tender sympathy, the thunder's voice is more glorious, the flowers are more pathetic. Even the jagged heights, the chasms and torrents, seem to enter the circle of human sympathies and claim kinship with him.

As the flowers bloom on the graves of those we love, so let our thoughts of them be fragrant with the cheerful spirit of faith and hope. Love reveals to us our infinite poverty — our boundless need of it, and our utter inability to reward the simplest soul who loves us. Inner strength, strength of mind, heart, and conscience, is human life, and the source of all that makes life precious and delightful. Hence the highest aim and end of education is to nourish and develop inner strength.

The more we live within ourselves, the richer and the more health-bringing will the current of our lives flow to others. If thou hast wealth, whether it be money or knowledge or virtue, it will become known. Work, in the doing of which it is impossible to think, is inferior and hurtful to prosperity of soul. It is the kind of work she does which gives to woman her greater delicacy, refinement, and insight; her more intimate consciousness of the worth of morality and religion, of beauty and love. Make no claims upon others; demand of them neither recognition nor appreciation nor gratitude, but trust in God and in thyself. The wrongs which we have done are like voices from heaven urging us to make them good. Hope and faith perish as they merge into love and knowledge; but they perish also when they merge into animal indifference and sensual indulgence. The more superior thou art, the less shalt thou be guided in the way of what is called happiness; and the more shalt thou be tried and afflicted, that through tribulation thou mayst be brought to deeper insight and purer love.

The radical soul-mood, in which feelings and emotions, experienced and repeated through years, have settled into permanence and consistency, and for which we have no proper word, determines more than all else our life and fate. Our opinions spring from the will rather than from intellectual views. We easily accept as we readily do what suits us, what is in harmony with our temperament and prejudices. We take the part of those we like, believing they are right, because we like them. We lean to the side of what is low or high, sensual or spiritual, in virtue of the law which draws like to like and kind to kind. They who care or care not for music or painting or poetry, or the beauties of nature or display, or delicious food and drink, are not swayed by logic, but by taste and feeling. For this reason teaching and preaching accomplish so little. We receive information and listen to arguments, but our soul-mood remains unchanged. Nothing is more disappointing than to expect good results from talking to people about what they do not or will not see for themselves. The truth which we receive mechanically, as we take a book from another's hand, is not truth for us. It is a mere formula; and it would be as wise to attempt to nourish the body with chemical formulas as to hope to strengthen and illumine the mind with words which are accepted, indeed, but not pondered and wrought into one's spiritual being.

It requires more ability and courage to think rightly than to act well. The power of seeing what we think of, of forming a mental image which brings the thing before the mind in distinct outlines and vivid colors, the true teacher will strive assiduously to develop and train. It gives a life and reality to thoughts and words which nothing else can impart to them. ·Who educates a boy, it is said, educates an individual; who educates a girl, educates a family. But it may happen that in educating a boy we help to educate a whole people. The possession of wealth gives a sense of security and independence; but intellectual and moral power alone can give the joy and peace which are blessedness.

Put from thee all pretentiousness, bear good will to all men, and learn, as far as this is possible, to do without them. In seeking to influence others it is easy to go astray; but in working for one's own intellectual and moral improvement, the way is plain and safe. Hadst thou been born and reared, surrounded and tempted, like the criminal who excites thy indignation, thou shouldst probably not be better than he. Apply this thought to whatever may prejudice thee, or make thee harsh in judging thy fellow-beings. Millions of human beings might be wiser and happier than they are; but attend thou to the two or three near thee whom thou mayst and shouldst make wiser and happier. Think not what thou wouldst do, hadst thou other powers and opportunities, but with what thou hast do what thou canst. " I have done what I could," he said, and his lips closed forever. The virtuous and the innocent

are patient and mild, and the truly religious are
meek and loving. God's knowledge could not
make Him happy, if it were not also love. He
who is sustained by strength of mind and heart
is great, and kings who lack this are weaklings.
Go thy way with a tranquil mind and without
haste; thou shalt reach the end just as surely as
though thou shouldst madly rush.

The divine message which the greatest men
have borne to the world is this, — Love truth
and be true to love. Doing and suffering are
the great teachers. They are, in fact, the only
creators of knowledge and power which God
has given to man.

Each one must feel wherein his talent and
vocation lie; for, in following this, he follows a
divine call, is self-impelled; and the self-impelled alone continue to be active and accomplish enduring work. The effort, not the success,
determines moral worth. Sorrow and disappointments make only the weak despondent
or bitter. Nature will not change her laws for
thee; learn then to understand and obey them.
God can give thee nothing so good as the love
of Himself. Self-sacrifice is the law of man's
life and development. He finds himself in
abandoning himself, in giving up the lower for
the higher, in devoting the present to make
possible a better future, which, in turn, when

it becomes the present, must be also sacrificed that something better may be attained.

Thus human life is aspiration, desire, and effort; a rising through faith and hope out of one's self toward the ideal of a nobler self. This is the way of progress from the helplessness and imbecility of childhood to the strength and wisdom of heroes and sages; this is the law of love, which in abandoning all finds all. This is religion, this is philosophy. So long as there are men who turn from themselves to a truer and diviner Self, so long shall there be those who love God and one another, who strive and toil, bear and suffer, that they may hasten the coming of the heavenly kingdom and the prevalence of the divine will on earth.

Religion is the atmosphere in which fathers and mothers and children, friends and lovers, breathe with freedom and true inward delight. It alone makes it possible for them to say and to feel that their union is eternal. It gives them simplicity and sincerity, mildness and patience, sympathy and helpfulness. What we suffer for becomes sacred to us: the child to the mother, his country to the soldier, his art to the man of genius, his work to every noble striver. Permit not thy faults to discourage thee; thou failest in many things; but if with a simple heart thou strivest to do well, it is well with thee. The higher thy service, and the greater the number of those whom thou servest, the nobler thy life. To pray or to read a book of devotion in a mechanical way, is not only not prayer, but, if habitual, it weakens the power of attention and undermines mental vigor. It is not only loss of time, but a hindrance to intellectual and moral growth. To be beautiful or intellectual or great, merely by contrast, is a poor thing; but to be beautiful or intellectual or great, in the company of the beautiful, the intellectual, and the great, is a divine thing. Put far from thee, then, jealousy and envy, knowing that the good of others heightens thy own.

In the tumult of the passions and of the life around us, it is difficult not to cease to be one's self, not to become the sport of chaotic elements; above all, is it difficult in the midst of this turmoil, to reach the serene heights where the soul sees God and lives for truth and love. Cultivate thy own field, employ thy own talent, live thy own life. If it should be thy lot to live in the midst of harsh, narrow, and unreasonable people, thou needst not be unhappy, if thou canst still see in them the elemental principles which make man worthy of sympathy and love.

Praise is most pleasing to the young and the frivolous. The love of it is a mark of immaturity, a proof that we are still standing on the lower rungs of the ladder which leads to true worth and honor. Egoism is foolishness; it comes of a lack of sense for relation and proportion; it is an inversion of the divine order of things. In jealousy there is a sense of inferiority. It is a mistake to speak of one's troubles; they are never interesting to others.

There is surely a ray of the Godhead in thoughts which wander through eternity, which embrace heaven and earth, which weigh the stars and compel remotest suns to deliver the secret of the elements of which they are composed. A true woman's love is more precious than the crowns of kings, than the wreaths wherewith the brow of genius is entwined. Bear, O woman! the divine gift in an immaculate heart; for God bestowed it that thou mightest raise and illumine souls, and make them feel that the All-powerful is also the All-loving.

We are born of God. In and with Him we live. To be separate from Him is not to be or to be nothing; to have conscious, permanent communion with Him, is to have eternal life. The miracle of miracles is a knowing, loving soul. The more we live within the mind, the more shadowy and unsubstantial the material world becomes for us, and the more independent we become of its tyrannic sway. Speak and write

what fills thee with peace and the sense of freedom which only truth can give. It will do thee
good, whether or not it bring light and solace to
any other soul.

It is hardly possible to be impartial with
one's self, for he who passes the judgment finds
himself, with all his ignorance and prejudice, in
the judgment. Hence the wise gladly hear
the honest opinions of others about themselves;
for through their eyes they may hope to see
themselves better than with their own. No one
owes thee praise; and if approval is bestowed
on thee, receive it not as thy due, but with
thankfulness as a gift. Rejoice in all the great
achievements of men and nations, whether or
not they seem to be in harmony with thy personal interests and opinions. The good feel
that the treasure-house of the race is not full
enough of noble deeds and words, and are unwilling that any precious thing which adds dignity to human nature should be lost sight of or
obscured. Look at great men, whether thou
knowest them in person or only in their words
and deeds, with admiration, but with an independent spirit, which stoops not to imitation,
but draws from such contemplation nourishment
and strength to lead its own life, to fulfil its
divinely given and self-appointed course. Live
in what is of universal interest, in what must be

considered good and true and right by all who
think in whatever age or land.   It is only
through the development of one's endowments
that it is possible to approach the ideal.   The
self-active can hardly fail to find their proper
work.   Since in human life there is no com-
pleteness, progress is the law of our being.   If
I carry aught beyond the grave, it must be the
thought and love with which I have lived so
long, and which is so much part of me, that,
without it, I should not be myself.   All else
may fall from me as the blossoms fall from the
tree; but if my thought and love should perish,
I should be no more.

The most unfavorable environment is not that
which prevents us from accomplishing anything
whatever, but that which hinders us from becoming true men and women.   Take many points
of view that thou mayst understand the many
ways in which the many kinds of men look at
the world.   So shalt thou come to see them not
through the mists of thy prejudices, but in the
light of their own thoughts.

If thou art busy upbuilding thine own being,
thou shalt easily learn to respect individuality
in others.   To the best larger freedom should
be conceded, but if they yield to the baser appetites they are not the best.   Blessed are they
who need nothing except God and their own

thoughts. Whoever has known the love of any
worthy man or woman can hardly think meanly
of human nature. A brave and cheerful spirit
makes the path of knowledge and virtue easy
and delightful. He who has found truth is not
disturbed by the noise and pomp with which
lies make their tours through the world, nor
does he look with envy on the palaces in which
their votaries dwell. Better doubt than pretend
to accept what thou knowest to be false. The
important consideration is not what or who is
seen, but who sees. O holy indifference to the
thousand things about which men fret and wear
themselves with worry! thou art half of life's
wisdom. Strong men experience a sense of
helplessness when they recall their early days
and feel that now they no longer have a father
or a mother to lean upon, while they themselves
have lost the power to open their whole heart
though a father and a mother were left to them.
What would they not give for one hour from
out the blessed time, when those cherished
beings sheltered them from even the shadow of
fear — God's providence made visible to love
and guide and watch over them. Belong neither to the school of the weeping philosophers
nor to that of the laughing, but let a brave and
cheerful spirit make thy life at once serious and
joyful. Expression has more charm than fea-

ture, because it is the symbol of one's spiritual life, while feature is but physical. A single virtue, if possessed in an heroic degree, though found in a character disfigured by faults, not only redeems its possessor from infamy, but makes him forever interesting. Whatever else the individual may sacrifice, he may not give up the right to develop his spiritual endowments, to grow in intellectual and moral power, for this would be to abandon the right to become and be human, to become and be a free and rational being. Whatever tends to reduce man's spiritual being to a state of inactivity, to an attitude of passiveness in the presence of the highest and holiest, is evil, and leads to the soul's destruction. To forbid to think and strive is to forbid to hope and love. What absolute value the human mind attributes to reason is manifest in the fact that all men, however opposite and contradictory their opinions and beliefs, appeal to reason to justify them. Facts themselves are facts only so far as reason accepts them as such. The immobility of the earth ceases to be a fact when reason declares that it is not a fact, but an illusion.

Why object that the thought I utter has been expressed by others? May I not praise the stars because their glory has been sung by the noblest poets? The faults of others displease us most when they are our own. If we could determine the course of man's life as we do that of a planet, he would be an unfree, wholly material being. Let not then human inconsistencies trouble thee, but rejoice rather that man's ways are incalculable.

If thou shouldst think that it is only probable that there is a God, or that truth and virtue are the best, do all thou canst, by action and meditation, to persuade thyself that this probability is a certainty; for to know and feel that God is and that He is truth and goodness, is strength and joy and peace. Weep not with Alexander, because there are no more worlds to conquer; nor with Heraclitus, over the miseries of mankind; but do thy work, learning day by day to do it with more perfect skill and thoroughness. If thou hast done good work, thou hast thy reward; but if thy work is poor, why shouldst thou be rewarded?

The hope that our labors shall at last lead us to rest and the tranquil enjoyment of life, is an incentive to effort, and therefore good, though delusive, since active minds are incapable of repose and the tranquil enjoyment of life. Whether consciousness is good or evil depends on what we are conscious of. For those who are conscious of only misery and pain, it is evil. He whose misfortunes are due to his principles and not to his passions is not without consolation. The secret of wisdom lies not in the six and twenty letters of the alphabet. If thou wouldst learn it thou must study life. There is the wonderment of children and of the crowd, and there is the wonder of great and noble minds, which is admiration, reverence, awe, and worship. They who are distinguished by circumstances alone have no real distinction at all. Since we do not know what life is, how shall we know what God is? It is enough that we know that He is and that He is the highest. Truth is absolute, so is goodness, so is beauty; but in the mind of man they can never exist as absolute. Truth for us is what we know. What God shall show to us in other worlds we can but surmise.

Higher knowledge and culture modify the form and intensity of our passions and needs, but leave them still with us. The truth which a man is capable of grasping depends on what he is. Wouldst thou teach higher truth? — strive to make higher men. Doers and endurers are wise and helpful, but mere talkers are a hindrance to their own and others' progress. We easily convert to our views those who have no views or only opinions, but with those who have convictions we generally labor in vain;

and when convictions are inseparable from
interests arguments against them are futile. To
overcome prejudice serves no good purpose
unless we at the same time cultivate love of
truth and nobleness of feeling. The habitual
attitude of the will toward the conscience is the
standard whereby character should be judged:
for no one always does well. There is no
greater blessedness than to know and love the
truth which the world turns from, as though it
were not worth a thought. Not by writing, but
by doing, not to be written about, but to be
wrought into life, was Christianity established.
Simplicity and sincerity, mildness and patience,
sympathy and helpfulness, are the characteris-
tics of the truly religious. Where there is
clamor, dispute, and controversy, neither the
spirit of truth nor the spirit of love will make a
home. Unity and self-possession, in thought,
word, and deed, are the mark of strength.
They constitute harmony, beauty, and power of
life. True thoughts and noble sentiments please
us because truth and nobleness are our element
wherein it is well with us. Love is our realm.
Where and wherein we love, we are kings,
crowned with joy and gladness. So long as we
love, so long see we God in His world; when
its flame is quenched the universe is but a char-
nel house. With love our happiness is born,

with love it dies. As a man's enemies help him, if he be a real man, to become stronger and wiser, so the foes of religion, of progress, of science, and of art should give us higher and juster views of them, and enable us to realize more fully their truth and beauty. The truer one's self-knowledge, the less anxious is he to appear, to play a part, for he feels that the important thing for him is to become and be a real man. It is well to live in the past and the future only in as much as we draw them both to the present to make it richer and fairer. Many things happen which might trouble me, but I escape from them in thinking how little of the infinite possible evil does happen. The thought that our misfortunes give pleasure to those who do not love us may make them harder to bear; but they who find satisfaction in the miseries of their fellowmen are not worth considering. The frivolity of our disputations is manifest in the swiftness with which they lose significance, so soon as the wheel of time brings up other issues and passions. We grow hot and breathless over trifles, while the divine interests of humanity leave us unmoved.

Let those who are able to descend into the depths of life and thought bring up, not slime, but pearls. Let there be light, is the cry of great souls; and they who diffuse the purest

light are the divinest men. Whoever has left
authentic record of his faith and hope, of his
yearning and love, of his joys and sorrows, of
his strivings and searchings, of his doubts and
struggles, is my benefactor; to me his memory
is sacred; I receive and hold his book with
reverence and gratitude. Leave each one his
touch of folly; it helps to lighten life's burden,
which, if he could see himself as he is, might
be too heavy to bear. In becoming there is
more joy than in being, as the promise is richer
than the fulfilment, the early morning sweeter
than the high noon. Think not of what thou
art or hast, but of thy infinite need of truth and
love. If they who think little of thee and thy
gifts are right, thou sufferest no loss; since
their opinions of thee neither diminish nor increase thy worth. They who find fault, however, help thee to know thyself, while they who
praise are apt to blind and lead thee astray.
National vaingloriousness is enrooted in personal vanity. Hence, when we show the base-
lessness of some general conceit, we give offence
to individuals, who seem to say to themselves,
if our nation is not the greatest and most enlightened, then we ourselves are not what we
think we are. The world wishes to be beguiled
with lies, it loves mock heroes and little great
men; but plodding truth, walking in the foot-

steps of time, sweeps away all mere rubbish. If thou art a true man, whether or what posterity shall think of thee will give thee no concern.

The worth of praise is measured by the worth of those who speak it. As a mere favorite may wear the insignia with which heroes are decorated, so ridiculous or base behavior may win honors, — honors bought with dishonor. Let the noblest achievements of men encourage, not dishearten thee ; let their crimes warn, not embolden thee. While I sit in my room beside the church, infants are brought for baptism, the betrothed come for the wedding, and the dead are borne to the funeral; and birth and marriage and death are so intermingled that they become but a single process, now rising and now sinking, as life's wheel turns. The thought that the one we love must die, accustoms us to death better than meditation on our own last end. In manhood, the fruit of life's tree may be ripe and wholesome, but the blossoms have fallen and all the garden has become less fair and fragrant. A glory has passed from the earth; and instead of the infinite heart of hope which made the youth like a god, there remains to the man but the fixed resolve to walk on in rough and narrow ways to the end. Well for him, if he lose not heart.

When thou hast done thy work thou hast done all thou needest do. Let others praise or make use of it, or in heedlessness or contempt pass it by. The course of nature, as it appears to us, is blind and senseless; and it is not conceivable that we shall ever be able to reconcile it with reason. Nothing is left us but to believe that God, in ways we cannot imagine, will make all things right. Such faith is possible, since we are the children of the Eternal, while our troubles and miseries are of a day. Good-will, magnanimity, and love are worth more than all the gifts of fortune.

Great thoughts, clothed in fitting words, are like a benediction from God. They raise our spirit and cheer and strengthen us in all our ways. To the words of genius, which are immortal, the printing-press has given a kind of omnipresence; and now they illumine and gladden the lovers of truth and beauty in all places, — whereas, of old, though they could not die, they could not live everywhere. They who excel in athletic sports excel but for a brief period; but they whom exercise of mind makes superior may behold, even in old age, victory wreathe her crown about their brows. To what class a true man belongs is of little moment, since a high and genuine personality rises above all classes into the sphere of pure humanity.

Pray God to deliver thee from the blindness which hinders thee from seeing truth and goodness in thy adversaries. If the mind languishes in the prison of ignorance and prejudice, the whole man, whatever his social or political environment, is enslaved. A free spirit is the root of liberty. Help men to become conscious of their spiritual being, that they may know God, whose image is reflected from the material universe, indeed, but only in and for the self-conscious soul. There are things which are accidentally interesting, and they command attention but for a time; there are others which touch the substance of life, and they have the power to entertain and delight wherever men think and strive. If thou wouldst be strong and free, let these be the daily nourishment of thy soul. If thy words and deeds give hope and heart to men, thy life will be precious to them, and they will cherish thy memory, as wanderers in the desert think with delight of the sparkling waters and green fields of fairer lands.

The maxim of ascetic writers — not to go forward is to recede — applies with special force to the mind. Not to learn is to forget, not to think is to weaken the power of thinking. When the multitude of writers lay hold of a truth, however divine, it loses vital power; in

passing through vulgar minds it seems to become like them. Be not provoked by what
shocks and rouses thee from mental somno-
lence, but awaken thy mind and exercise it,
that nothing may have power to disturb thee.
Only a growing soul is pleasing to God. If thou
hast not the heavenly gift, be thankful that thou
art able to recognize it in others. " Instead
of finding fault with Schiller and myself," said
Goethe, " our contemporaries should be glad to
have two such fellows as we." It takes a true
man to write a genuine book, and the best in it
is his own life, interfusing itself with all things,
and drawing from them nourishment and the
power to recreate them. Men of genius make
knowledge easy, but they do harm if they lead
us to imagine that we may acquire it without
the persistent effort by which alone the mind
is made capable of knowledge. The stamp
which genius sets on its noblest work is that it
serves no useful purpose. It grinds no corn to
nourish a perishable existence, but it lifts the
soul to realms of immortal life. What we live
by we rarely live for. When there is question
of the things which provide us with the means
of living we quickly cease to be believers and
lovers, to become partisans. He who lives not
for himself, not for money or fame or the good
opinion of others, but for truth, freedom, and

justice is great whether he accomplish much or nothing.

We visit gladly the places where man or nature produces what is excellent, or if we cannot visit the places we seek in some way to get possession of what is brought forth; but the noblest feel most keenly the need of the best that man has done. They crave for Homer's song more than for the wine of Chios. We are infinitely needy, and if we cannot be made to feel the need of truth and love, let us be thankful that we feel the need of better food, and clothing, and houses; for this will save us from a merely animal existence. If the work thou art able to do is mechanical, it may be provided for thee; but if it is spiritual, and is to have genuine worth, thou must find it for thyself. Let him who performs what is great or holy, be clean in body as in soul — the hero when he offers battle, the orator when he faces his audience, the priest when he ascends the altar.

He who teaches me new truth acquaints me with myself, by revealing a phase of my life, which was unknown to me. The best — strength of mind, purity of heart, and power of imagination — must be sought for itself simply because it is the best. The common man is preoccupied with thoughts of the means of living, and he imagines that he has no time to think of living. His mind, like his hands, or the soil he cultivates, is valuable to him merely for the practical uses to which it may be put. He who knows that he has divine gifts does not complain of lack of appreciation. He is lifted to worlds where the multitude is powerless, whether for praise or blame. If the praise of thy contemporaries give thee little pleasure, why shouldst thou be glad to be able to believe that a few hundred years hence, men will speak well of thee? Because thou feelest that the worth, which time does not destroy, is alone genuine. Great minds and heroic hearts conquer even in dying. Their spirit survives, and in the breasts of others wins victories. Much of what is spoken and written to stimulate the ambition and industry of our youth is false and hurtful. The burden of it all is that by labor, thrift, and honesty, they may get to be presidents, senators, millionnaires, widely known lawyers, physicians, and merchants. Their attention is directed to what is external, to what the unworthy may attain as well as the worthy, or to what very few can hope to reach, while the infinite wealth and blessedness of the inner world of thought and love is ignored or considered as a means, not an end. Thus, the tendency of the young to take delight in noise and display, the tendency of our national life to lay stress chiefly upon material progress and vulgar success, is fostered and intensified; the superstition that what a man possesses constitutes his worth and happiness is encouraged and sunk more deeply in the soul. It is a shallow philosophy which confuses popularity and riches with wisdom and virtue, one which will never form noble minds and characters. Happy is he whom neither the heat of youth nor the love of company, nor domestic cares nor a multiplicity of business, can wean from that inner world where man lives with high thoughts and images of divine beauty. The consciousness of possessing a power within ourselves which we feel to be good and pleasure-giving, and which struggles to realize itself in thoughts and deeds, is for each one the impulse to action and the source of achievement. Never dissatisfied, forever unsatisfied. The occasion shows the great man, because he brings to it the power of his whole past, alive with all he has believed and hoped, thought and done.

That which impedes, furthers the progress of the active and resolute, as water the fish's, air the bird's. The earth which draws us downward prevents us from falling as we walk. Our foes are our helpers: the passions which lead astray, impel, if rightly controlled, to heroic effort. There is not in this world anything so precious that to possess it a wise man will abandon the life of thought, or sacrifice peace and serenity of soul. If a fruit-tree should throw all its vitality into its roots, content with earth and the company of slimy things, and should never break into bud and flower and bear rich nourishment, it would be a proper image of the man whose thoughts and desires are given over to what is material and sensual. The wise and the virtuous shed blessings; their very presence illumines and purifies. To know is a certain good, to be known, a doubtful one. Live with thyself and thou shalt be at home, wherever thou art. " If thou wilt receive profit," says A'Kempis, " read with humility, simplicity, and faith; and seek not at any time the fame of being learned." To be fruitful, knowledge must mature amid storm and trial, striking its roots still deeper into the soul. What a man knows and experiences is himself, and if we would help him we must enable him to know and experience himself in a truer and nobler way, that becoming other he may feel himself a new man. No argument is needed to show the falseness of apothegms which weaken faith in the wisdom of virtue or in the worth of honest striving.

A wise man can suffer much, can suffer even to the end of life, with cheerfulness, if he but feel he is growing in strength of mind and heart. Far from believing that a single pain outweighs a hundred pleasures, he comes to feel that joy is born of pain; and he welcomes the pain for the wisdom it teaches; for wisdom is joy. Virtue is a thing in good earnest; in all else there is something frivolous and unreal. As the ring of the coin tells whether it is genuine, so a man's speech discovers his character. Great souls suffer in silence, for they know that deeds, not words, attest and vindicate worth. The best is a quiet and a busy life — still, but stirring, like the stars which seem at rest, but are forever moving. Sunlight ripens fruit, not by falling on it once, but by lingering over it day by day, week after week. So truth matures the mind, not with a single touch, but by abiding with it through long years.

There is no surer means of attaining higher knowledge than to keep alive within ourselves that which we already possess. Rules are leading-strings for those whose mind's eye is closed. Let them but open it, and they will see the truth alive which in the rule is dead.

If the time spent in trying to discover and reveal the errors of others were employed in learning to know and correct our own, the world would be reformed. He is great whose ideas the best minds receive and make their own. The best know there is nothing so precious as truth, nothing so fair as beauty, nothing so good as love: and if thou teachest higher truth, revealest diviner beauty, and makest purer love prevail, they will be thy friends, and thy life will diffuse itself through the lives of the noble from age to age.

The man of culture is wholly free from pretence; pretends neither to know nor believe, nor feel nor admire nor love; but in all these things he goes farther than his words would lead us to think. Life is the highest we know, and our aim therefore should be to attain the highest kind of life, which is at once knowledge, power, goodness, beauty, and love. "The earlier we indulge in thought and reflection," says Landor, "the longer do they last, and the more faithfully do they serve us. So far are they from shortening or debilitating our animal life, that they prolong and strengthen it greatly." Turn from what is hideous or revolting, whether in nature or in history, lest thy view of God's presence in the world be dimmed. One of the evils of the newspaper habit is that it holds the attention to what is vulgar or criminal. My own words and deeds may injure me: another's cannot.

We show gratitude to the dead by striving in their spirit to further their aims and to complete what they began but left unfinished. What happens within ourselves, not what takes place around us, forms our character and constitutes our worth. Our thoughts flow in the channels which our habits have fashioned, and we appreciate the qualities with which we are familiar, like the butcher, who when he needed a lawyer or a doctor, chose the fattest he could find. A man of learning without philosophy is, according to Kant, but a mathematical, historical, philological, geographical, or astronomical cyclops. He lacks an eye.

There are those who hold that it would be wrong to lie even to save the race from destruction, and who nevertheless heap up falsehoods to help a party to paltry victories. He who has a world view and the habit of thought, easily brings whatever he sees or hears or reads into harmony with the principles which underlie his conscious life. His mind revolves in obedience to higher laws around a fixed centre. To be more fearful of falling into error than eager to discover and proclaim truth is to have no influence. The world of thinkers loses sight of such an one, and moves on along winding ways to new knowledge and larger conquests. The error which we hold inquiringly, striving to find what element of fact there be in it, is worth more to us than the truth which we accept mechanically and retain with indifference. Think for thyself, for in this way alone is it possible for thee to have any real thought at all.

As the blind can have no proper notion of darkness, since they can have none of light, which is its correlative, so the ignorant cannot be made aware of their ignorance. To know a thing we must know its opposite. The only effective refutation of error is the making truth plain. Everything else is mistaken zeal or love of contention. He alone is a critic who takes the point of view of the author whom he appreciates, and resurveying the field tells us where he has succeeded and where he has failed. The wise and the foolish may speak the same things, but they are not the same, for the character of the speaker lends weight and meaning to his words. Nothing can atone for the lack of intellectual seriousness; where this is wanting, other gifts are vain. If thou hast a real mind, thou understandest that the applause of a world could not satisfy thee, nor its reprobation destroy thy confidence in thy own thoughts. If thou livest not by the work of thy hands, be a helper of those by the work of whose hands thou livest. Rouse not the anger of a multitude, though it be but a nest of wasps. The best speech is a form of action, and as good deeds bear repetition, so do true words.

The art of living lies largely in knowing how

to employ one's leisure, the use it is put to being the test of one's worth and culture. Art, as well as philosophy and poetry, is the fruit of leisure nobly employed. With the same materials we may build a home or a prison; and by the use of the same faculties we may make ourselves godlike or animal.

> I slept, and dreamed that life is beauty :
> I awoke, and saw that it is duty.

Truths which we cease to meditate quickly lose vital meaning for us. Be not ashamed to borrow truth, for the borrowing enriches thee, nor makes the lender poor. Thou canst not change the order of nature, but faith and love will illumine thy mind and change thy heart. If thy acquaintance with men is large, thou knowest some who are wicked and perverse or miserly and mean. Take heed lest thou use harsh words in speaking of them; for bitter speech will make thee bitter, and sweeping con-demnation of the worst offenders even springs from partial and narrow views. Be busy mak-ing right what is wrong in thy own life, and thou shalt learn to look with more kindly eyes upon thy fellows; for the evil in others irritates and annoys us, because we ourselves are weak and unloving.

Gentlemen are rarer than ladies, because it

takes more to make a gentleman than to make
a lady. The nobler and purer passions are the
most enduring and the most pleasure-giving.
They who study molecules and microbes find
that they may study them forever; and they
who enter the world of thought discover that it is
infinitely rich and full. If the virtuous but knew
how to make themselves amiable they would
conquer the world. A prudent man acts without talking about what he intends to do, never
threatens, and never wounds the self-esteem of
any one, least of all that of his inferiors. Those
who appear to be the servants of truth are often,
like other men, merely the slaves of their vani-
ties and ambitions. If we feel that ignorance is
our enemy, we shall easily learn how to overcome it. It is easy to find writings in which
there is sequence and continuity, but detached
thoughts, where there is both form and substance, are rare, and are for many a more helpful tonic than the even sweep of balanced and
harmonious periods. Who scatter thoughts sow
the seed of harvests, which others shall reap.
Everything has been said, Labruyère tells us;
and then proceeds to write a book, as though all
were still to say. It is delightful to feel that
one is wide awake and intelligent. A little self-
consciousness here is not offensive. We all
approve the pleasure which a talker or a writer

takes in giving pleasure to others. Give men time to recover from their faults, as the green fruit needs time to grow ripe. The words of disputants are like fog-horns which deafen and make us more conscious of the obscurity by which we are surrounded. Talent without will, the spur to tireless effort, avails little. In the young it is but a promise ; and if it develops it is impossible to know whether it will lead to honor or infamy. A boy of talent is like a colt of promise. There is hope that he shall win the prizes, but many accidents lie in the way; and more in the way of the boy than in that of the colt. There is perhaps worth in what thou dost ; but if it is unrecognized, console thyself by calling to mind the ages during which men saw the kettle boil and the lightning flash without learning the worth there is in steam and electricity. Writing, not printing, is the noblest invention. The press is but a developed pen.

CHAPTER V.

BOOKS.

Seek'st thou for bliss?
Lo! here it is —
In quiet nook,
With well loved book.

BOOKS are a world — they interest and amuse us; they speak to the mind and the heart; they divert from care and sorrow; they awaken the fancy and set the imagination afire. They take us round the globe, travel with us through every land, ready at a sign to recount the rise and fall of nations; they linger with us in quiet vales to tell the stories of happy lovers or to rechant the songs of poets. In the agora or the forum they crave our silence while Demosthenes hurls his fierce invective or Cicero marshals the stately phrases of his lofty discourse. They transform ruins and make them loom before us in all their early splendor; from battlefields where waves the ripening grain, they evoke contending armies with all the pomp and circumstance of war. They bring to us, while

we sit in our easy chair, before our own hearth-
fire, the men and women who have served
and ennobled mankind, — those who have
made history, founded religions, framed laws,
upbuilt states, created arts and sciences, taught
philosophies, withstood tyrants, and endured
infinitely.

They are many worlds — they take us back
to the paradisal home; they lead us to the
promised land. At their bidding blind Homer
grasps his harp and the Grecian hosts assemble
on the windy plains of Troy. The unyoked
steeds champ the golden grain beneath the starlit heavens. Hector falls before Achilles, and
Priam kisses the hand which slew his son, making us feel that thousands of years ago, as now,
love was more divine than strength, pity more
godlike than power. To whatever spot on
earth is memorable, books will take us. To
whoever is in any way capable of human life,
they bring refreshment and joy. In the endless
variety of races and individuals, of tastes and
opinions, they have wherewith to satisfy all. Is
there a world to which poets do not offer themselves as guides? They dip their pens in the
colors of the dawn and the twilight. The young
hear them chant the praises of immortal love;
the strong, the all-subduing power of will; the
old, the peace of restful death. They take our

every mood; they laugh, they weep, they mock; and suddenly they are afire with the courage of heroes, or are rapt in ecstasy with saints and martyrs. They are the trumpeters of patriots who battle for their country, and to nursing mothers they sing low lullabies.

In the presence of the tragedies which try great souls, they take us by the hand to show us that the innocent can suffer no wrong, and that a brave and loving heart is superior to whatever fate or senseless nature may inflict. They humanize all common things, entwining their tender thoughts about broken toys and vacant chairs and locks of faded hair. The bucket that hangs in the well, the deserted house, with its door ajar, the path choked with weeds, whisper to them of joys and sorrows, of effort and failure, of life and death. Whatever hope or despair, faith or doubt, love or hate, ecstasy or agony, has touched a mortal, lies in books, immortal. All that men have planned and done, all that they have dared and borne, — their dreams and errors, their gropings and wanderings, their searchings for what others have found after they themselves had crumbled to dust, the miserable outcome of mighty undertakings, the vast results of insignificant beginnings, the rise of obscure tribes to world power, the sinking of great nations into nothingness, — all this lies in books.   They are for every age, for every type, for every mood.

On this wintry night I see a million glowing hearth-fires.   Around gentle mothers are gathered the sweet faces of pure children, rising head above head like the steps of winding stairs; and in the vision I behold books open, while fresh and all-believing souls look out through gray and blue and brown eyes upon them.   These are magicians who show things incredible.   Here are the thousand tales of wonder, — Aladdin with his lamp, Fortunatus with his wishing cap, Queen Mab and her fairy world, and Mother Goose, best of all.   Here are stories of wanderings afar, of adventures on sea and land, of the discovery of new worlds, of shipwreck on unknown islands.   Here are songs and melodies which mothers sang to their children a thousand years ago; legends which for young hearts never grow old, of King Arthur and his knights, of Robin Hood and his good men, of Bruce and Wallace and William Tell.   To think of it all is to be a child again.   The long procession of the years vanishes; the toil and the trouble, the sin and the sorrow, the promise and the perjury, are no more.   The world is fresh as on the primal day.   Whatever the seasons bring is newly dropt from the hand of God.   Death is but a dream, and life is all.   We are alive, and so are our fathers and mothers, our brothers and sisters; the whole world is alive, the brooks and the birds, the gardens and the fields, and the days are long, and filled with light. We drink the perfume, we bask in the sunshine, and are at one with lambs and colts and sucking pigs. We dance with the waving corn; with leaves we whisper foolish things to the mysterious air.

If some morning we awake and find the hills hoar with frost, what is it but a new kind of life? Our young hearts leap forth to the flocking snowflakes as gleefully as to spring showers; and when we see the wide white cloth spread we know it is for a feast. We hear sleighbells jingle, we see laughing eyes gleaming from close-drawn hoods, we listen to the crackling fire, we watch the roasting apples, the popping corn; the cider is amber in the glass, the nuts are cracked, and kings and millionnaires are melancholy fools compared with us. Are not the stars gleaming in the crisp air? Is not the crystal ice glistening on streams fallen asleep? And what is that uplighting all the east, but the moon, pushing away the darkness that she may look upon our glee? On the polished steel we glide, curving as bends the river, and the silent hills are glad, re-echoing our merry shout and laugh; the naked boughs catch the thrill of life, and dream of spring, — of leaves and flowers and songs of birds, of sweet girls and smiling babes, in whose eyes the azure skies are mirrored. Ah! welladay, all this was, but is no more. Thievish time has stolen our world, and where shall we find it again but in memory made quick by the noble spirits who speak to us from books, happy that souls are still alive who are able to partake their joys?

When we move upward and the breath of life becomes more intense, when the bud of youth and maidenhood is become a full-blown flower, and we feel the throb of universal life, the stirring within ourselves of the universal power which clothes all things with strength and beauty, when we long for the desert as a dwelling-place, with one fair spirit for a minister, where shall we find nourishment for the blissful mood, if not in books? In them all divine lovers become our companions. They linger with us to speak of immortal ecstasies, as they who love, love to talk of their love. Where shall we begin? In paradise, with the hymn of the first man smitten by the charm of woman's beauty? Or shall we pause to watch the conflict of Europe with Asia, sung by Homer, and all because of love? Or shall we hear Vergil sing how Love threw himself in vain athwart the way wherein moved the destiny of Rome?

Ah! well, the god was avenged, when the Power which denied love, having overcome the world, sank in the mire of mere animalism and was trampled by avenging hordes. Rather let us take no thought where we alight in the fair kingdom of fresh and tender hearts, for wherever we set foot books will welcome us and be our guides. Though we follow Dante to hell, the voice of Francesca shall make us dream it is Paradise. Shall we sit with Jessica on the violet-clad and moonlit bank and listen to the music in our hearts, or shall we lend ear to Juliet while she upbraids the hasty and officious dawn, that comes to drive from her the light and life that lie in Romeo's eyes?

Lo! it is St. Agnes' eve — the owl for all his feathers is a-cold, the hare limps trembling through the frozen grass, and suddenly upon our ears bursts the argent revelry, and we behold fair Madeline and Porphyro, who long ages ago fled away into the storm and were rich and rich enough with only love! Or shall we turn aside to weep with Isabella over her basil pot? For hearts aflame with love, books are full of tales of love. Like bees in clover fields they may light anywhere and sip nectar. Alas! we may there also see the men who might have towered in the van of all the world, let occasion die while they did sleep in Love's Elysium. But

for the young, in whom life's pulse most deeply
throbs, love is but an episode. They dwell with
thoughts and hopes which are athrill with heroic
daring and endurance. They are straitened in
the world and lack breathing room. They
would discover new lands, build states, strike
tyrants down, break the chains of slaves, lead
captives into promised lands, and stand in the
front of peoples, like saviors, to deliver them
from ignorance and sensuality. What a world
of noble books there is for them, from that
which tells of Abraham, who went forth from
his own, leaving that which had intertwined
itself with the tenderest fibres of his heart, that
he might found a new race and build a kingdom
of God, to that in which we behold Lincoln,
much enduring and much hoping man, trusting
in God and in right-loving and right-discerning
souls, until he saw his country emerge from the
sea of blood, undivided though sorrow-crowned,
to resume her divinely appointed mission to
spread freedom and good-will among all peoples.
But we may choose from any age or land, for,
thanks to the heart which makes us men, those
who greatly dare and do and suffer, have never
anywhere been lacking.

There is Plutarch, name worthy of homage,
who makes it possible for us to live with the
founders of states, the warriors, orators, and

poets, the men of power and genius, who were Greece and Rome. What is history but the biographies of great men, of those whom courage, faith, and industry have made leaders of the people and doers of memorable things? The value of such books lies largely in the enthusiasm which they inspire. They who loved justice and freedom, who for their love suffered exile, ignominy, and death, rise before us as we read their story, to bid us look away from present and apparent success, to the world of enduring things, where the wise and true, whether in life they wandered homeless and friendless or suffered the punishment of criminals, have ascended to the worth and power which cannot pass away.

For those who know how to read, history teaches as nothing else can, that a human soul, centred, in truth and right, is invincible, acts with the power of God, and like Him, prevails. But to youthful minds its pages do not make this lesson plain. They are drawn to deeds of prowess, to the flash of the orator's thought and the thunder of his voice, to the poet's song of glory and triumph, to the power of the law-giver and the thinker which tames savages, and brings reason and conscience to play upon the affairs of men. They read with the heart and the imagination; they do not yet understand what labor it costs to learn how to read as great minds read. They are hungry for sensation. They look eagerly on the panorama of nature as it unfolds itself in books, more intelligibly and more enchantingly than to the senses, for they, like all the heedless, have eyes and see not, ears and hear not. They look on the starlit heavens and think it a common sight; for them the stars are but pimples on the face of the sky; but with books as their guides they learn to find themselves at home in interstellar spaces, and perceive that the earth is but a minor rock, a mere spall, lost amid countless solar systems. Caught in the meshes of the senses, they think the little circle in which they move, in city or in village or amid the fields, a world, as it is, indeed, their world; but when they come to see themselves in books as in mirrors, they see how less than nothing is the baby world in which they have been living, — a mere fool's paradise. Their knowledge, their thoughts and deeds, have seemed to them to be of weight, to possess a power which is unrecognized; but when they have gone deeper into books, what they know becomes ignorance and what they do sheer vanity. Thus young readers, if they are destined to make themselves a home in the world of books, are taught first of all the wisdom of modesty. If they cannot learn this, the use and worth of books must remain hidden from them. So long as we live in the realm of mere happenings, real or imaginary, we live on the surface of things, and are still controlled by the instincts of barbarians. We are spectators who are fascinated by the glitter, and movement of life, like children who take delight in foolish games or are carried beyond themselves by the sight of what is strange. A toy is more interesting than a thought to those who are incapable of thought.

In the plays of the great dramatists, it is the story and not the poetry which gives pleasure. The perfect phrase, the utterance of deep wisdom, retards the action, which alone interests the multitude of spectators. Hence the noblest plays are rarely put on the stage, and as rarely read. Profound writers have few readers. It is not possible that they should interest those who live amid the shows of things and are more eager to listen to gossip than to words of wisdom. In books as in all things we seek ourselves. Narcissus-like we see in the stream of matter but the reflection of our own countenance, and when we look up to the eternal and infinite we still see our own image. In our money, our country, our friends, we love ourselves. In her child the mother finds the symbol of her virginal love, which made the world a paradise; in the lullabies she sings, she hears far-off echoes of her maiden dreams. Hence each one believes and feels that the best books are the books in which he finds himself. For a whole world of rosy cheeks and bright eyes Mother Goose is better than Plato or Shakspere; and for a world a little older Robinson Crusoe has more worth than all the philosophies.

A boy will read a tale of adventure, but not a history of scientific research; a girl a story of love, but not a treatise on womanly virtue. Why urge your favorite dish or tipple on those by whom it is disliked? What suits us suits us, and there is an end of the matter. No, it is not so. On the contrary, it is the business of life to give us an opportunity to learn to know and love the best things. When we are children we take delight in the things of children; when we become men we still feel the charm of our early existence, but the childish has no longer power to please us. Having become other we cease to be able to find ourselves in the haunts of the olden times. They are beautiful to memory, but had we to go back to them we should find them unendurable. We cannot love the highest unless we see it; and it can be seen only by those who make themselves high. Books are not everything, but for those who wish to lead the higher life they are indispensable. "Whosoever," says De Bury, "acknowledges himself to be a zealous lover of truth, of happiness, of wisdom, of science, or even of the faith, must of necessity make himself a lover of books."

Whether we wish to live in the past, or to forecast the future, or to fill the present with delightful thoughts and images; whether we wish to gain a knowledge of law, or of medicine, or of theology; whether we wish to listen to the philosophers, or the orators, or the poets, to weep over tragedies or to laugh at comedies, or to thrill at the spectacle of the heroic struggles of patriots and martyrs; whether we wish to learn how to live or how to die, — books must be our teachers. If we seek knowledge, they will impart it, if counsel, they will give it; if we want consolation, we shall find it in them, if recreation and beguilement, in them also. They are athrill with life, and the best of them being alive now some thousand years, inspire us with thoughts of immortality; and since though old they are still young, they have the power even when age bears us down, to rouse within us the fresh hope and courage of youth. "I would not barter my books and my love of reading," said Fénelon, "for kingdoms and empires." "My early and invincible love of reading," said Gibbon, "I would not exchange for the treasures of India." Cicero declared that he would

part with all he possessed rather than not be permitted to live and die among his books. When
Scott, returning to Abbotsford to die, was
wheeled into his library, the tears burst forth;
and Southey, no longer able to read, loved to
kiss and stroke his books.

As we cannot fathom the wealth of life there
is in a real man by occasional conversations
with him, so we cannot appreciate the worth of
a genuine book by simply reading it. We must
study it, learn to know it as we know a friend,
seek its company and return to it again and
again, with expectant and joyful hearts, as we
return to those we love. There are not many
books which are worthy of such devotion, nor
will all of these commend themselves to all.
Each one must find for himself those he needs,
those which stimulate him most; one or two, at
least, which are precious to him he must discover, or remain inferior, never attaining true
insight into the worth and beauty of life. The
important thing is not what we like, but what
we ought to like, questions of taste, like all questions, being questions of reason. One of our
chief aims should be to form purer and higher
tastes. The worse pleases us because we have
not accustomed ourselves to the better. The
saying — tell me what you eat, and I will tell
you what you are — is true certainly of our spir-

itual nourishment. They who feed on low thoughts and desires are low men.

The best thing the youth carries from college is not knowledge, but the ardent desire to learn; and the best knowledge he gets in school is the knowledge of how to learn. Genuine books inspire faith and courage, confirm hope, beguile sorrow, teach wisdom, fill the memory with beautiful and noble thoughts, thrill the heart with heroic aspiration, sow the mind with the seeds of truth, bring the distant and the past, with all their glories, victories, failures, and defeats, to the homes of even the poor and heavy laden, to enrich, soothe, and enlighten their weary and lonely lives. If parents, teachers, and priests would but take the trouble to get definite knowledge concerning the books which are best suited to rouse the young to mental and moral activity, and if then they would wisely direct and encourage them in their reading, they would doubtless render them higher and more lasting service than any which may result from their admonitions, lessons, and exhortations. But children are left to grope their way or are permitted to read whatever chance or the family or public library throws into their hands; and since their judgment and taste are unformed, it is more than probable that what is false and vicious will please them rather than what is genuine and good. The end of reading, as of whatever else we do, is self-improvement. The world exists for man, and its proper use is to make him more fully man. Books then are but a means of self-culture. They help us to think, to believe, to love, and to do, or they render us no service. Books which impart information are superseded as knowledge increases, but books into which genius has poured its soul, keep forever, each its distinct place, in the world's literature. As they sprang from deep glowing minds and hearts they retain always the power to awaken and strengthen minds and hearts. They remain as a spiritual presence, to move men to diviner sympathies, to lift their thoughts to more enduring worlds. Their creators

" Shake the ashes of the grave aside
  From their calm locks, and undiscomfited
  Look steadfast truths against time's changing mask."

A work of art, like " Hamlet " or " Faust," which may be had for a few cents, would be held above all price, if, like the Sistine Madonna or the Transfiguration, its perfect truth and beauty could be found but in a single exemplar. The book-lover, hidden and unknown, may feel that all the mighty men of words and deeds are his servants. For his delight and instruction, they have thought and written and conquered and upbuilt. To him they re-sing their songs; to him they rehearse the story of their struggles and triumphs.

He who leaves a fortune leaves it to be wasted or misused; but he who leaves a genuine book, leaves a precious and imperishable heritage to all the wise of all the ages to come. What we need to make us what we are capable of becoming is not new information, but a new impulse which shall rouse us to a fuller consciousness of the infinite worth of truth and goodness, and this impulse is given by the vital books, the books of power. A library teaches at once the vanity and the nobleness of human life. Here lie the thoughts, hopes, dreams, joys, sorrows, ambitions, and works of a thousand minds, desiccated and labelled, like specimens in a museum. Into this mummy dust they have all crumbled. And yet what divine virtue must there not have been in these hearts, whose words, after the sleep of centuries, are ever ready to awaken to thrill the living with a new sense of the deathless power of truth and beauty? How is it possible to dwell here and not be pure, humble, and reverent, or not feel the godlike worth of man's thought and love? And have not those who have lived affectionately among books been in general good and deserving men? "The love of study," says Gibbon, " a passion which derives fresh vigor from enjoyment, supplies each day, each hour with a perpetual source of independent and rational pleasure."

If conversation lag I find my friend is dull; but if I take up a book which I know to be full of inspiration and power, and it prove uninteresting, I am driven to confess that the fault lies in myself. Thus books, being unchangeable, are touchstones whereby to prove ourselves. An author who suggests, enlightens and instructs also; for to be impelled to think is to be impelled toward insight and knowledge. The greatest thinkers even have left us but fragments of their minds, or if they have written what seems to be a complete transcript of their inner world, that in it which we find inspiring and helpful is fragmentary, for in the world of books, as in that of men, we choose and love but what suits our taste. The higher our intellectual power and culture, the more clearly do we perceive how few there are who are capable of grasping the thought and import of a great book. In the words of the Saviour, simple and plain as they are, how much there is which the multitude have not yet fathomed; nay, which philosophers even have failed to understand in all their divine significance and truth!

For the right appreciation of literature, it is not sufficient to have a cultivated mind or a pure heart or a living power of imagination, but we must have them all and have them act in harmony. The evils which the habit of reading what is inferior entails, are serious. It wastes time which might be profitably employed; it leads to inattention, since poor writing invites the mind to wander, having in itself no attractiveness; it prevents the development of a taste for what is excellent, enfeebles the power of discernment, dulls the edge of the intellect, and accustoms one to content himself with the superficial and the commonplace. Its effects are similar to those which are produced by association with the foolish and the vulgar. "I hate books," said Rousseau; "they teach us only to talk about what we do not know." This is true of those who read but the books of facts; it is not true of those who read the books of power. It is not difficult to find those who are indifferent to books or who have a distaste for them. Shut such an one in a library, and he is as lonely as if he were confined in a prison cell. For him the books are as dead as the walls; their presence may even irritate him and add to his wretchedness. He stays gladly with men or horses or flowers, but books are as melancholy as tombs: they give him a sense of discomfort as though they were haunted, having heard, perchance, that there is some sort of mysterious presence in them. It is the man or woman, the brave, generous, thinking soul we find in the book, which makes it precious, makes it a friend. But magazines and newspapers, like corporations, like the syndicates that publish them, are soulless. They merely represent something or nothing, like a member of Congress, whom we hardly think of as a man. A book, like a living person, may inspire love or hate; but who can love or hate magazines or newspapers? They are idle things for the idle and for idle hours. They have no power to take firm hold of us and to rouse us to self-activity. They have no character themselves, and are therefore powerless to form minds and hearts. They are for the moment, and their readers live aimlessly in the present. Their world is what happened yesterday or an hour ago, and their educational value is not greater than that of gossip and other trivial pastimes; but since they touch upon everything, those whose reading is confined to them, talk about many things, understanding nothing. Put your daily newspaper aside for a week and then look through all the numbers, and you will need no argument to prove of how much valuable time it robs you. The newspaper reader lives in a crowd, in the midst of a mob almost; and in such environment it is difficult not to lose the sense of responsibility or to retain a sense of refinement, decency, and self-respect. He becomes callous both to what is noble and to what is vile. The deeds of heroes do not move him, and crimes and calamities only in as much as they minister to his passion for novelty. He is capable even of a semi-conscious longing for wars, famines, floods, and wrecks, that his craving for news may be fed. He tends to become like the Roman multitude, whom the sight of men butchering one another made drunk with pleasure. The houses of the powerful and the rich may be closed against us, but if we are lovers of books, we feel that we are the equals of the best, for we live in the company of prophets and apostles, of philosophers and poets. Socrates will ask us questions, Plato will admit us to his garden, and Cicero, lying at ease in his Tusculan Villa, will discourse to us of all high things.

> I rode with Milton all day long,
>   With Milton at his best;
> He sang his high heroic song,
>   While I reclined at rest.

" O thou who art able to write a book," says Carlyle, " which once in two centuries or oftener there is a man gifted to do, envy not him whom they name City-builder, and inexpressibly pity him whom they name Conqueror, or City-burner." In the library of even a poor man we may easily find a company of the wisest and wittiest, gathered from many lands and ages, for his instruction and entertainment. He need but put on his wishing-cap and any one of them will begin to talk or sing.

A genuine book, like the sun, has heat and light enough for all the world through all the ages; nor does it lose what it gives, but though it have nourished and delighted a hundred generations it still retains the power to fill a hundred more with strength and joy. He who has not learned to find pleasure in some one of the great books, of which all have heard, will not profit by making inquiry concerning what he should read; for he who loves none of the great books reads to little purpose.

"Books," says Channing, "are the true levellers." But this is doubtful praise. The aim should be not to bring all men to a common level, but to lift as many as possible to all attainable heights, that the multitude may be drawn to follow them. There is no merit in equality, unless it be equality with the best. Strive to make thyself like God, not like the crowd. A good book delights me the more when I think of all the pleasure it gave its author, of all the joy and consolation it has given to thousands. It is like a jewel which has become more precious for having sparkled on the breasts of fair and noble women. A book is not genuine unless it can be read again and again, even after the lapse of years, with new profit and delight. That which having read we care not to look at a second time, is an ephemeral thing, and should have been printed, if at all, in a newspaper. " He that walketh with the wise," says Solomon, " shall be wise." He who converseth with the best books shall be strengthened and purified.

Great minds are distinguished by power and depth rather than by newness of thought. They write what all may understand, but what they alone possess in its fulness and freshness. The truth which others passively accept, they lay hold on and work into the innermost fibres of their being. It pursues them and gives them no rest, for however they strive to utter it they feel that it is still unuttered. They perceive, as none else, its surpassing worth and application to life ; and it is their faith in its beneficent and purifying power which constitutes their genius, and which more than the beauty wherewith they clothe it, gives it attractiveness and arrests attention, for when readers find in an author who does not lack ability profound conviction and seriousness, they are persuaded there must be something in him deserving study. Their interest is thus awakened, and among many a few will be found who will labor with earnest-ness and perseverance to master his secret. Genuinely great minds in the presence of the thought and faith which express the highest and holiest intuitions and yearnings of the soul are reverent and devout; and whoever treats these subjects with flippancy, banishes himself from the company of the best. It is his lack of reverence and devoutness which makes it impossible to class Emerson with the great teachers. As it takes a hero to know a hero, so it takes a true reader to know a genuine book. A book from which I can gain nothing has no value for me; but if it is one in which others have found profit, its failure to help me is probably my own fault. It happens that a volume which we put aside as uninteresting, will, if taken up in another mood, or when study has reformed our judgment and taste, prove to be of genuine worth and service. At all events, it is certain that books which are the expression of the experience, thought, hope, faith, and as-piration of real men, are fountains of living waters for all who know how to draw from them. A book which makes us contented and thank-ful, resolute to bear up under adverse fortune, and to continue bravely struggling, which confirms our faith in virtue and in knowledge, and our trust in God, is good and wholesome, whatever its faults.

> "We get no good
> By being ungenerous even to a book."

Brilliant qualities will not secure a permanent place in literature for a writer whose thought does not reach the inner core of truth. "Truth illuminates and gives joy," says Arnold, "and it is by the bond of joy, not of pleasure, that men's spirits are indissolubly held." Generous sentiments, wide views, a tranquil and enlightened mind, a tolerant and sympathetic nature, free from anger, envy, and all pettiness, create the spiritual atmosphere which writers who are destined to immortality breathe. What is best in the genuine books is neither ancient nor modern. It is the work of minds who, rising from out the lapses of time, utter what is eternally true and fair. The great books belong to those alone who have souls akin to the minds whose thought and love they hold; give them to kings and presidents, and they find them to be only so much paper and morocco.

If we take a survey of the classical authors, poets, philosophers, historians, and orators, and note their most striking passages, we shall be impressed by the sameness of thought and sentiment which runs through them all, and thus

we shall get a deeper insight into the narrow-
ness of the circle in which even the noblest
minds are condemned to move.   Again and
again, from age to age, from Greece to Italy,
from Jerusalem, Athens, and Rome, the same
truth emerges, clothed almost in the same words.
Genius itself despairs of uttering anything really
new, and the man of genius, while recognizing
that the best has already been said, is tempted
to lament his late appearance on earth.   The
more familiar we are with the world's literature,
the more clearly do we perceive, that apart
from new theories, resulting from new discoveries, inventions, and happenings, there is little
any one can say which is new.   But the soul
of man, being infinite in its aspirations, capable
of thoughts which transcend all bounds and
penetrate eternity, is never weary of contemplating the spiritual facts which constitute its being,
and which, like itself, are of unfathomable import; and therefore it never loses relish for the
old truth, which is forever new in its applica-
tions to life, having power, like light, to remain
itself, while it clothes the world with endless
variety and beauty.   Hence the works of genius
never grow obsolete, but flourish from generation to generation, bearing fresh flowers and
rich fruit; and as no truth is exactly the same
for any two minds, so is truth modified to suit

the changing environment in which the race lives, now emerging with diviner power and significance, and now obscured by the passions or the heedlessness of the age. But to him who has once perceived its real nature, its infinite worth is plain. He will abandon all, if need be, to follow it. It is the pearl above price; it is joy and love. It leads to the inner world where consciousness reveals God and the soul. It makes us meek and lowly, merciful and lovers of peace; it fills us with longing for righteousness; it enables us to bear patiently persecution, poverty, and obloquy, for these affect the outer man, not him who lives within, whom truth makes free and a citizen of unseen and higher worlds, capable of the spiritual worship, whereby he recognizes his kinship with the Eternal and with all the pure and loving souls for whom the universe is a temple and God is all in all.

Since the multitude of men love to see things happen and to talk and read of them as happening, but have little capacity and less liking for reflection, it is not to be expected that they will read books which are interesting only because they rouse the intellect and compel thought. Such books will not find many readers, but the few who study them will outweigh in mental force and moral worth whole millions who relish nothing but stories and newspapers. Though we be not able clearly to perceive the priceless treasures stored in books, let the testimony of so many of the noblest minds persuade us of their worth, and inspire us to discover for ourselves the marvellous world of which these immortal spirits have left such good report. Shakspere's advice, to study what we most affect, has worth, but may easily mislead, for most readers are pleased with what is inferior or vicious, whereas the aim of whoever wishes to improve himself should be to learn to take delight in the best. A taste for what is genuine in literature, as a taste for what is genuine in art, being an acquired taste, a main purpose of our reading should be to cultivate the power of distinguishing between what is genuine and what is spurious. In genuine books we may often find things which we cannot accept, which repel us even; but this will not prevent the earnest student from striving to get at what good there is in them. The greatest writers have their faults, and no one author teaches the whole truth. Intellectual progress, in fact, is a process of choosing from the best what is suited to our needs.

The reading as the writing of books may be a disease, the indulgence of morbid propensities, of vanity, of indolence, of a fondness for what is sensational or frivolous; and it is doubtless true that many of us spend no time more idly than that which we give to reading, which unless it rouse us to self-activity, does us harm. The case with speculative and practical truth is the same, — neither is vitally held except by those who cease not from striving to learn, whether by thinking or by doing. As it is better to know a great man than to hear others talk about him, however pleasant their discourse, so is it more profitable to study genuine books than to read about them. Literary criticism is valuable only when it wakens in us a desire to acquaint ourselves with the books which thrill with life and power; for to them and not to the critics we must go for light and strength. In writers who have merely talent thou shalt vainly look for help. If thy mind is to be made luminous and the fountain of thy heart opened, it must be done by thoughts which spring from the deepest soul of man. All of worth which even the best writer has to impart is derived from his experience; but his experience, to be interesting and fruitful, must be communicated with the tact and skill, the correctness and adequacy, the ease and grace, which constitute the charm of a real man of letters. Reading is valuable chiefly as a stimulus to action, since the end of life is to do rather than to think. Hence what fails to rouse within us courage and the impulse to act, helps us not at all or little.

Beware of words — there is no worse delusion than that which leads us to imagine that the acceptance of the same formulas is equivalent to a union of mind and heart. Words are but symbols, and to attempt to substitute them for truth is preposterous. This verbal superstition is the more to be dreaded, because great writers have such mastery over language that their readers easily mistake the form for the sub- stance, and worship an idol instead of God. Men rush into all kinds of danger and folly, rather than bear the imputation of cowardice or superstition, so great is the tyranny of words over unthinking minds.

The reading of many books gives pleasure, but the careful study of a few profits most.

> " Who reads
> Incessantly, and to his reading brings not
> A spirit and judgment equal or superior,
> Uncertain and unsettled still remains,
> Deep versed in books and shallow in himself."

However well an author express his thought, it is not possible for him to impart the experi- ence without which it cannot be rightly under- stood. As the mind grows, the aspect of things changes, as objects seen through a microscope appear other than when viewed with the naked eye. Mental culture leads us to worlds unlike that in which we grew up, — as much wider and richer than it as our modern universe is vaster and in every way more glorious than the one the ancients imagined. As our fuller insight into the laws of nature is the result of the labor of centuries and of innumerable minds, so the individual can acquire culture only by industry and observation, by patient thought and much reading; but once it is ours the pains it has cost are forgotten in the sense of freedom and strength which it imparts. "Culture," says Arnold, "is indispensably necessary, and culture is reading, but reading with a purpose to guide it, and with system. He does a good work who does anything to help this; indeed, it is the one essential service now to be rendered to education." Read with a dictionary at your side, and never pass a word whose meaning you do not fully understand.

Most readers seek themselves in books, but an awakened mind finds all the books in himself — they but serve to call his attention to the fact that they are there. When a young student enters a great library, he is overcome by a sense of discouragement. How shall he ever learn all the wisdom which is there stored? The labor of a lifetime must still leave him on the threshold. But one who is master in the art of reading knows that a few books, thoroughly assimilated, are a key to all others, and he no more dreams of reading them all than of eating all the provisions in the market-house. Their chief use is to nourish, strengthen, and inspire, and but one in thousands has vital substance.

Original authors are rarely found interesting at first; they rather repel and give pain because they call forth in the reader the consciousness of his inferiority. But if he persevere, he learns to love them for the help he finds in them. Love indeed is the only thing which can put us at ease with the truly great, for it alone makes us glad to acknowledge their superiority. There is no author, as there is no man, who is wholly great. The best are great only on occasion or in setting forth special phases of truth, when they are fully themselves and throw all their power of thought and feeling into the matter. The reader's secret is to know when the diviner mind speaks, and to wait upon its utterance with thoroughly awakened attention, passing lightly over what is ordinary and uninspired. He seeks in each author for what he can find in him alone or at the least more perfectly in him than in any other. As a good workman does good work even with poor tools, so a true reader finds intimations of truth and beauty in books in

which others see nothing. He carries himself
to the task, and reads his own mind into and out
of the printed page. It is not by hearing elo-
quent men or by visiting strange lands and
venerable monuments, that we shall come to
insight which they alone attain who dwell with
their own thoughts and make the godward
ascent from their own hearts.

"I hate this shallow Americanism," says
Emerson, "which hopes to get rich by credit, to
get knowledge by raps on midnight tables, to
learn the economy of the mind by phrenology,
or to acquire skill without study or mastery
without apprenticeship." The only essentially
interesting things in the world are the struggles
of men for knowledge, liberty, and virtue, and
the most pathetic thing is the blind and helpless
way in which they struggle. Here is America,
set apart and dedicated to freedom, peopled by
a chosen race, and it is already delivered into
the hands of mammonites, Philistines, boodlers,
thugs, and editors. How shall we have faith in
the power of man to govern himself and to upbuild his being to the full height? The wicked
who love not their fellowmen, but study how
they may dominate and make use of them, trust
to nothing so much as to the dulness, inattention,
and sensual indolence of the multitude. If the
inert mass could be lifted to the plane where

men think and care, all reforms would be made easy.

When we fail to recognize the truly great, the loss is ours, not theirs. The knowledge of books which the most have is like one's acquaintance with a chance companion. We remember that he said this or that, but the spirit and heart of the man is hidden from us.

The book is suggestive, but what does it suggest to the dull and heedless? The universe is athrill with truth and beauty, but for the multitude it means little more than bread and meat. Read what gives thee delight, thrills thee with admiration, and awakens love; but strive assiduously so to form thy judgment and taste that only the best shall please thee. The important thing for thee is not what divine truths may be found in the works of men of genius, but what thou findest in thy own mind and heart. There or nowhere is the infinite life revealed to thee. The best authors are not those who teach most, but those who inspire the love of excellence, and give their readers strength and courage to pursue it with perseverance.

> The noble deed, the perfect word,
> Undying works, is ever heard.

It is easy to find fault: appreciation requires intelligence and character.

" We have a combat to sustain," says St. Basil ; " to prepare ourselves for it we must seek the company of the poets, the historians, and the orators." Play at games when thou canst not find a genuine book or a true man to entertain and enlighten thee. A little volume will hold the wisdom of mankind, but it is wisdom only for those whom reflection and experience have made wise. Carlyle and his disciples have striven to persuade us that genuine faith is not possible in the present age, which they believe hopelessly given over to insincerity and cant. It is a shallow doctrine, and one which the grim seer, whose eye was quick to pierce shams, should have plainly seen to be an unreality. The universe has not fallen to decay, nor have the brain and heart of man withered. God is in His heaven, and the world is as glorious as on the primal day. Man knows more than he has ever known, he is freer, more human and stronger than he has ever been; and it is childish to take the tone of complaint in the presence of our wider views, deeper insight, and aims more consciously worthy. The world is indeed, as it has ever been, full of insincerity, since wholly true and genuine natures are and always have been rare. This is part of the mystery of evil which we cannot fathom, but which does not weaken the faith and hope of brave hearts. The evil there is in men is plain to the dullest. The wise study the good there is in them. Thou lovest, O my soul, blue heavens and white clouds up-piled, the starry vault and moonlit sky, plain and snowy peak. Thou lovest the race of man, to which all saints and sages, heroes and poets, belong; of which are born the nursing mothers whose faces bend over sleeping infants, smiling in their sleep, watching over them until they grow to fair maidens whose thoughts are sweet and pure as flowers new blown, to youths whose hearts are fresh and strong as torrents leaping adown their rocky beds. This is God's world, my soul! thou art His child; have no fear whether thou wake or whether thou fall asleep.

In literature nothing really counts but that which sane and honest minds have written in uttermost sincerity; the rest is like a dress of ceremony which suits the occasion, but has no further use or significance. In the best literature even we feel that words fail to reveal truth and beauty, whose very nature it is to elude expression. Whether we write or paint or chisel, we pursue what cannot be overtaken; but the futility of the highest effort is recognized only by the most sincere and poetic souls. The common man is content with his common achievements. The books which never lose their power to charm are those which reflect the very life and mind of their authors: for a living soul is perennially interesting. No writer, however much genius he may have, is great, if his spirit is perverse. The affinity of the mind is with truth, goodness, and beauty, as that of the eye with light, and a fondness for the darker sides of life is evidence of perversity. The noblest influence is that which inspires the love of truth and right. So averse is the spiritual from the sensual nature, that the preservation of the individual and the propagation of the race seem insufficient to bind the soul to this servitude, and hence it is prodded with the goad of appetite and lust, until stooping to the mire its bedraggled wings can hardly lift it again to the azure dome. Shall genius turn traitor to the soul, and become the purveyor of putridity?

The art which is at all times within the reach of all is found only in books. If one could easily meet with men and women who are at once intelligent and sympathetic, their company might be as pleasant and possibly as helpful as intercourse with books. But since such society is hardly to be had, how gladly one flees the ceaseless din of talk of one's self and one's neighbor, of politics and business, of marriage and death, to take refuge with the noble minds, who, emancipated from the bondage of earthly life, dwell in the serene world of immortal things. A word or a hint shows the whole matter to intelligent readers. At a glance they see the author's scope, and decide whether or not he is worth studying. In quitting one book for another, as in leaving one person for another, we often feel not only that we have crossed oceans and ages, but that we have gotten into other worlds. Take thy book as thy money. If with it thou canst please and help others, be glad; but, if they care not for it, it is not therefore the less precious to thyself.

What a delightful thing it is to come upon a book scarcely known, in which there is the breath of genius. I can recall the time when I measured my progress in learning by the size of my class-book; and there are many I believe who do not think that great wisdom may be found in a little volume. It is like the prejudice against small men, or the notion that great men should have high place or live in a large city. When they speak of a little book they imply that it has little worth. A genuine book is a mirror in which we behold our proper countenance; but if we ourselves are unsightly, how shall we hope to see the reflection of a face clothed with beauty? He who gets from books only what they contain, knows not their proper use. The best service to be had from them is not the information they impart, but the exercise of mind to which they impel. Many imagine that when an author is declared to be an atheist, a materialist, or a pantheist all that it is necessary to know of him has been said; but real minds strive to get at the thought of real minds, whatever their world-view be. The phrase does not determine the thought, but springs from it; and if we wish to understand how well an author writes we must look first to what he intends to say. When the substance is known, the fitness of the expression is easily perceived.

To have a conception which will not issue into light and form, and to struggle with it till the right word and the right phrase reveal themselves, and the thought springs forth like Minerva from the brain of Jove — this is to experience the creative force of genius. In every good style there is a quality which gives it vitality and charm, and which cannot be acquired, but is inborn. It is like the tone of voice, the manner and expression, which stamp one as a distinct individual. If the thought is clear and high, it will clothe itself in fit words. Inferior style implies inferior thinking. One might suggest Kant as an objection, but the last thing which may be asserted of his style is that it is inferior. Goethe said that to read him was like entering a well-lighted room.

Confine thy reading to books which inspire and illumine, or give information on subjects in which a serious mind may take genuine interest. The time we give to newspapers would, if rightly used, bring us to philosophical insight. If a masterpiece, consecrated by the consent of the competent, please thee not, be silent. To condemn were folly, to praise, insincerity. The plaintive tone, which seems to rise from the depths of despair, sounding like the murmurs Dante heard escaping from the pool of Malebolge, and which is frequent in the writings of Renan and other religious sceptics, is a false note in literature. The author has not the right to be weak and cowardly, and if such knowledge as he has been able to get, takes from him hope and heart, he will hardly persuade us that it has worth.

The best books have given most delight to their authors. How gladly Plutarch lives among his heroes and sages; with what cheerful contentment Montaigne makes his book, feeling that thereby he is making himself; into what a serene world the Emperor Marcus rises when he writes his thoughts! Plato has the spirit and light-heartedness of a healthful youth; Chaucer rhymes his tales as merrily as birds trill their matin songs ; and to turn to minds more intense, Dante and Milton forget their exile and blindness, while they sing of the eternal abodes of men, and of eternal light and darkness. Bacon is like a mediciner, gathering healing herbs in flowery meads; and Descartes, for whom the hidden life is the good life, sat quietly looking into his own mind and into nature, until all things were clothed for him with intelligibleness. Defoe is happy on his desert island, St. Pierre would linger always with his youthful lovers, and À'Kempis leads forever his devout and simple life.

They who utter original thought are single and alone: but for right minds they are more interesting than warriors with their armies, than kings with their pomp and circumstance; and the interest they inspire endures while right minds endure. The most beautiful thoughts spring from remembered things which in far-off days mellowed the soul and suffused it with light. They are like the wine which rose within the grapes of springs long gone, and which through years has grown rich and fragrant in cool and hidden cellars. There is a flavor in them which nothing but the hallowing influence of time and sorrow can give. They are filled with the colors of dawns and sunsets, they are redolent of showers and dews; there is in them the odor of new-ploughed ground, and faint echoes of the laughter of children and of

the lullabies of mothers rocking their babes to
sleep. The whole earth is made fair and spiritual by the monuments and works of art, which
all know, whether or not they have seen them.
In thinking of Jerusalem, Athens, and Rome,
we become more conscious of the divine element in humanity. They are symbols of what
our race is worth. In the same way a man of
genius, though we know of him scarcely more
than his name, ennobles us all. To these
heights, we say to ourselves, one of our kind
has ascended; we are not of base blood since
we have such a brother. To read a book with
the understanding merely is to miss its true
significance and power ; for a genuine book is
written by the whole man, and contains not
merely what he knows, but it is athrill with
what he thinks, dreams, imagines, hopes, believes, and loves. It is his living vesture woven
by himself out of the substance of God and all
things.

They do not read books who complain of the
endless making of books. A true reader is willing that thousands appear, if but one of them
has worth, as the miner gladly throws up tons
of earth, if here and there he find a precious
stone. How is it possible to live without literature, without intercourse with books, without
nourishment for the spirit which makes us men?

If thou findest nothing new in the book, it has at least helped thee to see how wise thou art. The *vae soli* does not apply to those who think, for they live with the truth which makes the universe alive with God's presence. O Genius, sell not thy gifts to the rich and powerful nor yet to the rabble. They were bestowed upon thee by God, for godlike uses. "Books," says Hazlitt, "let us into the souls of men and lay open to us the secrets of our own. They are the first and last, the most homefelt, the most heartfelt of all our enjoyments."

We boast of having talked with a great poet or philosopher, whose books lie unopened on our shelves; and yet the conversation was commonplace, while what there was of genius in the man lives in these dust-covered volumes. If we could go to the tomb of a divine man and wake him and bid him speak, we should set the world agape and all men would be eager to listen. His book is his tomb, where he lies asleep, ready, if we wish, to shake off his slumber and tell us the best he knew and loved. As it is well to turn the young loose in gardens and fields, to permit them to wander in woods, over hills, and along flowing streams, so is it wise to place in their hands the best books, helping them to choose what pleases the fancy, quickens thought, raises the imagination, and purifies the heart. To say that we are responsible for what we read is but to say that we are responsible for what we think and do, love and admire, hope and believe. Books make readers, as opportunities provoke endowments. They are opportunities for spiritual growth. In them we discover not gold and precious stones, but ourselves lifted into the light and warmth of all that man knows and God has revealed. To read the best books it is not enough to be attentive. We must linger in meditation over their pages, as in studying a work of art or a beautiful landscape, we love to stand in silence before it, that so, if possible, we may drink its life and spirit.

CHAPTER VI.

THE TEACHER AND THE SCHOOL.

The godlike man, the noble pedagogue,
Who cast a people in heroic mould. —GOETHE.

PUBLIC education is a people's deliberate effort to form a nobler race of men. It is of paramount importance, because other things which the national life fosters, as growth of population, increase of wealth, abundance of food, comfort, facility of travel and transportation, political, social, and religious freedom, are but means to the one end of human effort, which is to make man himself wise, strong, loving, reverent, pure, and fair. India and China have half the population of the earth, but we care not for them, because their life is unintelligent, unprogressive, and uninteresting. We look to kind more than to numbers and magnitude. Microbes are more numerous than men, trees are larger.

When we consider the universal stream of matter, the human race appears to be of little more importance than the insect tribes which fill the air of a summer evening. The earth spins on in its double whirl, the stars gleam, the heat glows, the rain falls, the rivers flow, the seasons come and go, bringing life and death to the children of men as though they were but flowers which bloom in the morning and die at evening. But when we deepen our view, we perceive that the thought and love of man give to matter its spiritual element, its truth and beauty ; and that he therefore is of a higher order and of more worth than all the orbs which fill the limitless expanse of the heavens. In the same way, when we look at the human race itself, the individual appears to be insignificant; but when we come closer we are made aware that it is the individual who guides the mass to weal or woe. He founds religions, moulds heterogeneous tribes into nations, creates civilization, art, literature, and science. He undermines faith and hope, or uplifts and holds the multitude to the consciousness of God's presence in the world and in the soul. The race forms the individual, the individual gives rank and importance to the race, which exists and acts only in and through him. Hence the highest function which a people can perform is to assist the individuals of which it is composed, to bring forth within themselves the qualities which make them human, which make them true and good and fair and wise. This is each one's life-task, which is never finished, for it means ceaseless effort, strong and great-hearted striving for the best. This is what religious minds teach when they tell us that it is man's duty to grow like to God, — God who is power, wisdom, and love, in unimaginable excellence, the perfect being, the highest of which it is possible to think. This is what philosophers affirm when they declare that a man's proper business is to make himself reasonable, virtuous, and humane, that he may become self-active in the service of truth, beauty, and goodness. The ideal is human perfection ; the means whereby it is approached is self-activity. We are men only so far as we are self-active. It is this that makes us capable of thinking, observing, and feeling; it is this that gives us power to speak, to do, and to control our action. It is by rousing us to self-activity that God and nature work upon us, and it is by doing this that the teacher educates. The activity which nature, when left to itself, calls forth, is chiefly physical and animal. Savage tribes have dwelt from immemorial ages beneath the splendors of sun and moon, have seen the dawn and the gloaming and the starlit heavens, have walked by the sounding ocean and by wide rivers, have looked on the glories with which the seasons clothe the mountains and the plains, and yet their spiritual nature has remained untouched. They have continued to lead the lower life, groping in the darkness of ignorance and passion. It is not possible to give what we have not, and as nature is without thought and love, it cannot, of itself, awaken thought and love. This only the thinking mind and loving heart can do. Only they who are developed, educated, and formed, can develop, educate, and form others. Each one's educational influence is measured by the knowledge and culture which he has made his own ; and since knowledge and culture are vital and genuine in those alone who strive seriously and with perseverance to improve themselves, it follows that only they are true educators who are all the while busy upbuilding their own being, by increasing their power of knowing and doing, by deepening and purifying their power of hoping and believing and loving. No good work is ever done by men who do not put their heart in the work. Best work is possible only to those who take more delight in doing the thing well, thoroughly well, than in any reward they may receive. Men of genius create masterpieces because they throw their whole life into the task, believe in it and love it with all their might, heedless of what impression it may make upon others. Their art is for them a religion, an integrant part of their being, in which if they do not live, they die altogether. They never cease to strive, because they are guided and ruled by an ideal of perfection to which, however great their gifts or their performance, they never attain. They feel that they may yet do better things, and hope and confidence keep them fresh and strong. They *become* and find themselves in their work. They grow with it, and rise with it toward the truth and beauty of which it is the symbol and expression. Though every teacher cannot have genius, every real educator works in this spirit. He is a lover of human perfection in himself and in others, and he has a living and abiding faith in education as the great means whereby this highest end may be attained. Reflection and experience have taught him that what he is, is of vastly more worth and import than what he knows; that it is not his knowledge, his eloquence, his tact and skill, which are the true educational forces, but himself, his mind, his character, his will. If the young are to be led to yearn for learning, and to become self-active in the pursuit of excellence, his personality more than his words must be their inspiration and guide. If in the matter of education they are to be believers, and not infidels, their faith must be fed and sustained by his own. If he hopes to inspire them with high and generous sentiments, he must trust to his life, rather than to his words. Truth and goodness are life, and they propagate themselves only through the lives of those in whom they have become incorporate. The believer makes believers, the striver makes strivers, the lover makes lovers. The orator, it was said of old, is a good man who is skilful in speech. The educator, we may say, is a good man who loves human perfection, and who with faith and hope and tender patience labors to bring it forth in himself and in his disciples. He must be a genuine believer in education, in its power to uplift and transform men. He must cherish it for this power, that is, for itself; and unless he work in this spirit, he may be a trainer, but not an educator.

The question of education is much simpler than we imagine, and most of what is written and spoken on the subject serves but to obscure that which is plain. Its object is to produce vigor and activity of body, mind, and conscience. To this end the whole process of teaching and discipline should be made subservient. In the primary stage, up to the age of fourteen, the leading idea should be nutrition of feeling. Help the child to see and hear and feel; to wonder, admire, and revere; to believe, hope, and love. The whole material world lies open

for those who know how to look and listen;
awe, admiration, and reverence are elementary
feelings which touch the source of all higher
life; faith, hope, and love are the living waters
wherein young souls delight to bathe. Power
of believing is the measure of human power.
Israel believed in God, Greece in culture, Rome
in law, more than any other people that has
existed; and for this reason they have played
the chief rôles in the history of the race, and are
still alive wherever men think and strive for
better things. In the real sense of the word,
truth is never learned at school; but minds
rightly educated there, learn it later through
their own self-activity and through experience of
life. Whatever the child is taught, whether it
be reading or writing or arithmetic, or something else, has educational value only in as much
as it rouses and develops his spiritual nature.
There is no abstract education as there is no
abstract love. It is a process of life, a contact
of living beings, acting and reacting upon one
another. We may train a child as we train an
animal, but when our work is done, we have only
a trained animal. If we would make him a man,
we must teach him to look and listen, to admire
and revere, to think and will and love. Far
more depends on what we love and what we
hate, on what we hope and believe, admire and

revere, than on what we think and know. Education itself is promoted by willing rather than by knowing. He who has a live steadfast will to learn and love whatever is high and true and good and fair, has within himself the principle and power from which education proceeds ; and they who rouse and strengthen the will to strive through a lifetime for truth and justice and freedom and light, alone deserve the name of teachers. How can we will that of which we are ignorant? Through faith, through an instinct akin to that which leads the herd to springs that lie hidden in the midst of deserts; and to awaken and guide this is the teacher's great task.

There are ideas and sentiments and aims and hopes, which are held to be true and good by all men. They lie at the root of human life and character, and to turn from them in the process of education is not to educate but to pervert. He who awakens and confirms the faith of his pupils in the priceless worth of intellectual and moral power is the best educator; for thus he turns all their energies to the life-work of self-education. This is the highest aim, for whoever is self-active in learning and doing what is true and good and beautiful, in his private as in his public life, has education, and continues to educate himself. It is impossible to desire that of which we feel no need; and one cannot rouse the young to faith in the supreme worth of knowledge and virtue except by making them conscious of their infinite need of them. Shall we hope to entertain with accounts of the heroic struggles of the great and good those whose only idea of pleasure is sensual and brutal? Shall a prize-fighter take interest in a philosopher; a mammonite, in a poet? Desire begets desire, hope inspires hope, faith creates faith; and if the teacher is to be an educator, he must be a striver for knowledge and virtue, a lover of human perfection, a believer in the efficacy of rightly directed effort. Example has greater educational value than any possible verbal instruction, and a wise, strong, cheerful, patient, punctual, and loving man or woman in the school can do more than a consummate orator could accomplish there. As the mind is the man, so the teacher is the school, the material structure being comparatively unimportant. The greatest educator who has appeared on earth instructed and formed his disciples while he walked along lonely roads, or while he sat by the well or on the hillside, or while he stood in the bow of a fisherman's boat. And Socrates, the world-teacher whom we place next to him, taught wherever he found hearers, whether on the street corner or in the gymna-

sium or on the public highway. Such a teacher,
too, was St. Paul, the great heroic heart
whose deep and awful conviction of the life-
giving and indispensable nature of truth had
made him truth's bondsman. Give the right
man or the right woman a log cabin, and divine
work shall be done; place formal and callous
teachers in marble palaces, and they shall be
caught all the more hopelessly in the machine
which destroys life. In taking visitors through
our towns we point with pride to our imposing
school buildings. We are like rich men who
show their libraries, that they may boast of the
binding of the books and the editions de luxe.
Here, if anywhere, we should look not at the
vessel, but examine its contents. The great
house concerns us little, the kind of life found
and fostered there is the all in all, and of this
the material structure can give us no proper
conception; or may I not say that these large
buildings, where five hundred or a thousand
children are gathered, are a hindrance to the
work of teachers and pupils? Whoever has
driven through our Western States has noticed
the little schoolhouse, standing alone in the
corner of a field. There is not a tree to shelter
it, not a flower to smile upon it. The farmer's
barn half a mile away is more finely built, and
stands on a more favorable site. Do he and his

neighbors give more thought to the breeding and raising of cattle than to the education of their children, as they are more attentive to the strain where there is question of their domestic animals than where their own offspring are concerned? It may be so. At all events, that little schoolhouse, hardly bigger than a dry-goods box, above which no bough waves, around which no flower blooms, near which no brook flows, is as it stands there by the dusty or muddy road, in solitude and nakedness, weather-beaten and discolored, a better place for education, whether we consider the teacher or the pupils, than one of our great factory-like structures.

It is in the country; and it is better, where there is question of health and growth of body and mind, to be a country boy and to be allowed to play with freedom about the face of nature in all her moods, than to be the nursling of a palace in a great city, just as it is better, from the educator's point of view, to study the habits of an insect, even, than to gaze at the display in a shop window. The closer we come to nature the nearer we approach the source whence spring life and truth.

In cities education is most difficult. City populations are decadent, and would die out if they were not reinforced from the country.

There the home, which is the fountain-head of the life of a civilized people, is less potent and less sacred. Parental authority is undermined. Fathers and mothers, seeing that their influence is weakened by their environment, become careless, and since the State provides free schools they throw the responsibility for their children's education upon the State, and flatter themselves that in sending them to school they have done their duty. They, who are the true God-appointed teachers, neglect their office, and, like all the neglectful and incompetent, they are quick to find fault with others. They inculcate respect for the school neither by word nor example; and therefore the authority which the State has assumed, and which they have gladly delegated to it, its teachers are unable properly to exercise. In abandoning the care of their children's education, they give up all thought of their own. The primary duties of the family are not performed, and the family degenerates. The children are idle, unpunctual, and heedless. Their attendance is irregular, and the average for the school is low. The teachers are at a disadvantage. Their classes are overcrowded; they find neither respect nor appreciation, and since they see that the parents take no genuine interest in the education of their children, they feel that they labor in vain. It is futile to strive to awaken a desire for knowledge and virtue in those whom conceit or callousness makes self-satisfied. They find it impossible to perform their tasks with glad hearts and fresh hopes, like sowers and reapers who sing at their work; and they must have exceptional courage if they do not sink to the level of drudges and hirelings. Thring says that the life of many teachers may be compared to that of a man digging, knee-deep, in a muddy ditch, with banks high enough to shut out the landscape, in a hot sun, with a permanent swarm of flies and gnats around his head.

We are, doubtless, far away from the time when the pedagogue was a slave, far from the later ages when he was paid and treated no better than the lowest menial. It has, indeed, become the fashion to extol, in sonorous phrase, the dignity and importance of the teacher's calling. We recall with pleasure the names by which it has been made illustrious. Did not the Saviour of men teach as well as he wrought? Socrates, Plato, and Aristotle, Seneca and Quintilian, St. Augustine and St. Thomas of Aquinas, Bossuet and Fénelon, Milton and Locke, Kant and Hegel, — immortal names, who dwelt upon the summits of intellectual and moral power, were teachers. In truth all great men are teachers, in word or deed. The hero, the saint, the philosopher, the poet, the orator, the statesman, the warrior, whether by their example or by their utterances, rouse men from sluggish and animal life to high thoughts and aims, to noble sentiments and resolves. They are leaders in the way of progress, and from the heights which they have ascended, athwart innumerable obstacles, their voices ring out to cheer those who struggle in the plains below.

In the present century education has become a science, and teaching an art as well as a profession. The schoolmaster has risen to the rank of the physician, the lawyer, and the minister of religion. The social importance of his function is widely recognized, and the public, it would seem, looks, theoretically at least, with more favor upon him than upon the physician, or the lawyer, or the minister of religion. He is believed to be more unquestionably a public benefactor. He is a developer and shaper of life and destiny, and, as Horace Mann says, " One right former is worth a thousand reformers." It is indeed difficult to exaggerate the worth of a true teacher, of one who, loving children with a love akin to that which glowed in the divine heart of Christ, is wise and strong, watchful and patient; who, while he awakens and holds attention is able to enter the child mind to make it active and conscious of itself by rousing the thousand images of truth and beauty which slumber there; who has faith in education, and knows how to inspire his pupils with a genuine belief in it, as the one power given to man whereby he may lift himself to higher and higher planes of life; who, being a genuine lover of human perfection, strives to make himself as well as them perfect in body, mind, and heart. One who approaches, even, such an ideal, would be God-like, would be a glory, not of his profession only, but of his country and his race. The profession does not honor the man, but the man the profession; nor does the profession disgrace the man, but the man the profession.

But lest we lose ourselves in the contemplation of the ideal, let us descend and draw closer to the facts of life. No serious thinker who has given attention to pedagogics, will deny the importance of right methods, of good text-books, and of a proper choice of the subjects to be taught, in the light of the relative educational values of the different branches of knowledge; and if one should permit himself to be controlled by what he reads and hears in books and magazines and meetings devoted to questions of education, he would be led to believe that these and like matters are of primary and paramount importance. This would be a fatal error. It is, in fact, an error as widespread as it is fatal, one which obscures the central fact, and leads away from vital truth into quagmires and quicksands. Methods and other devices are mechanical, and machinery is as powerless to educate as to propagate life. One of our worst superstitions is the belief that we can develop, strengthen, and ennoble mankind by machinery and by talk about machinery, and so we argue about it and about it, and keep far away from the inner source from which all life and truth and goodness proceed. Mechanical minds are the cause of half our woe and misery, and we have all had opportunity to observe that they who most abound in words have little depth of thought, little strength of conviction, little power of will.

The teacher is the school. What the soul is to the body, what the mind is to the man, that the teacher is to the school. A good teacher will find or devise good methods, and will employ them with discernment, dealing with each pupil as an individual soul, unlike any other that exists or has existed. His very presence commands attention, solicits interest, and suggests thought. He is alive, and he awakens life. His pupils learn to feel that it is good to be where he is, and they follow him as gladly as though he led them into the balmy air of spring along the flowery banks of limpid streams.

The question of education is a question of teachers; and the problem to be solved is how to induce the best men and women to become schoolmasters and schoolmistresses; for such men and women alone can do good work, whether in primary schools or in colleges or in universities. They are as indispensable for the child who is learning to read and write as for the youth who is studying science and philosophy. In every stage of the educational process development of faculty, strength, and skill are the object, while knowledge is secondary. The teacher must know how to deal with human minds, and his chief concern, therefore, can never be with imparting anything to them, however valuable it be, but his study must be how to open them to the light, how to give them flexibility, how to make them attentive and self-active. His work is a wrestling of mind with mind, and of heart with heart; and if he simply drills his class as a whole he fails as a teacher. He is a trainer and not an educator.

If the teacher's labor is important and sacred, his task is severe, his calling hard. To remain vigilant and alert, hour after hour, day

15

after day, for months at a time, is wearying and exhausting. To be always in active contact with crude minds, some of whom, whether from inheritance or from neglect and vicious habits, are almost uneducable, wears the nerves and puts one's powers of patience and endurance to the test. In the midst of such an environment the fire of enthusiasm goes out and freshness of spirit is lost. The lawyer, the physician, and the minister of religion are less constantly occupied; their time is more their own, they work in a wider field, they are cheered by brighter prospects, they are more in the public eye, more sure of recognition and appreciation, are better protected from insolence and contumely, and their labors are better paid. It is needless to speak of the more enticing allurements which trade and commerce offer. How, in the face of all this, shall we hope that the most aspiring, the most active, and the most capable minds among our young men and young women will choose teaching as their calling? If we except a few eager and brilliant natures who will climb and sparkle, whatever their occupation or profession may be, what hope of advancement is there for the tens of thousands of the teachers of our common schools? Or if advancement is possible, is it not so uncertain or so slow or so inconsiderable that it stirs no glad anticipations? Teachers, like all of us, must live on hope, and if their calling gives them little nourishment for hope they will look away from it to some more promising source of joy and happiness. Teaching will not be followed as a vocation, as a life-work, but as an expedient. Why is there an almost total lack of male teachers in our primary schools? Is it not because young men understand that while the teacher's task is severe and ungrateful, his reward of whatever kind is smaller than that of other professional men, insignificant, if compared with what he might expect in becoming a politician or a merchant or a banker? Why are nine-tenths of the teachers in the primary schools women? Is it not because they, being either shut out from the other professions or finding access to them very difficult, and being unable for the most part to become politicians or merchants or bankers, are driven by the force of circumstances into the schools? And then, though their salaries are small, they earn better wages as teachers than they would receive for most other kinds of work which women do. Women rarely get the same pay as men for the same work. This doubtless is chiefly due to their exclusion from so many occupations, which results in an over-supply wherever there is a demand for their work.

Whatever the cause may be, the fact is that in the fields in which large numbers of women are employed, labor is cheap; and it is the cheapness of their labor, and not their superiority as teachers, which makes competition with them for positions in our primary schools so difficult. That this is a very grave evil is obvious. They who are content to accept cheap work in the school can have no idea of the meaning of education. They would degrade it to a mechanical process, and imagine that the teacher does his whole duty when he makes his pupils learn to read and write, and gives them some knowledge of arithmetic, geography, and history. They believe that those who pass an examination and show that they know enough to do this are worthy to be intrusted with the teacher's office. They fail to see that the important thing in the primary, as in every other school, is not what the child learns, but development of faculty and acquisition of habits. If he is made active in his spiritual nature, his mind will become supple and vigorous as the body is made supple and vigorous by exercise. Being makes action possible, and the kind of being determines the kind of action. The intellectually active alone can rouse the intellect, the morally active the conscience, the religiously active the soul. The lower cannot call

forth the higher. He who is not a thinker cannot make others think, who is not a lover cannot make others love, who is not a doer cannot
make others do. A liar cannot teach truth, nor
a boor gentlemanlike behavior. If we are to
have good schools we must fill our homes of
education with such men and women as we
desire our children to become.

The teacher's personality far more than his
learning determines his value as an educator.
The very presence of a brave, noble, generous,
and cheerful man illumines and strengthens.
He compels recognition and obedience though
he neither speak nor command, and they who
have known him never lose faith in human
nature, or in the worth of knowledge and
virtue.

The ideal, to have educational power, must
gleam through the concrete. The ethical ideal
is the ideally ethical man, the intellectual ideal,
the ideally intellectual man, the religious ideal,
the ideally religious man. If we would move
and influence the young in a profound and
lasting way, let us acquaint them with the ideal
incarnate in the persons of the teachers whom
we place over them. But how shall we hope to
make approach to this end, if we look upon the
teacher as a piece of mechanism whose cheapness is an important consideration?

All schemes, plans, systems, and methods prove futile in the hands of the incompetent. Inferior teachers make inferior schools. An educated man is never boastful, nor is an educated people; but if we must extol ourselves, let us remember that hitherto the school has been but an incidental factor in our progress. Much of it is due to the spirit of our race, much to our Christian homes, much to the churches, much to the conditions of a new country, in which freedom and unlimited opportunity stimulate to self-activity, much to the fact that the young and the enterprising have for more than half a century been coming from Europe in multitudes to our shores. Professor Laurie, who is a competent and an impartial judge, says: " America is an uneducated country as we now understand education. It possesses no national system; it has not even the machinery whereby education could be given in the sense in which it is given in Great Britain or Germany." Listen to the conversation which one may hear on the street or in the cars, read the newspapers of our towns and of some of our great cities even, and it will be difficult to deny that there is at least a degree of truth in this assertion. Corrupt and incorrect language means that there is no education or a faulty education. Debased speech is evidence of debased mind. Inaccuracy

proves that the powers of attention and observation, which it is the purpose of the school to
cultivate, are undeveloped. The lack of patience,
of perseverance, of faith in the power of obstinate and long-continued effort to transform one's
being, the absence of the nobler kinds of ambition, in our young men especially, are proof
that in the school their higher nature has not
been touched and made self-active.

It is a happy omen when the best minds in a
nation occupy themselves seriously with questions of education. This is what happened in
Germany at the close of the last, and in the
early part of the present century. Kant,
Goethe, Fichte, Wilhelm von Humboldt, Richter, Krause, Herbart, and other men of genius
or talent threw themselves into the subject
with enthusiastic zeal and confidence. The
result was a reawakening of the people, a rebirth
of the national spirit, and a general desire for
broader and deeper culture.

With us the school question seems to be a
matter of interest chiefly to declaimers and
politicians, who make it a popular cry wherewith
to drown the voices of earnest and enlightened
thinkers. They rally round the little schoolhouse, plant the flag on it, and, like Barbara
Frietchie, look out the window expecting to see
the waving of rebel banners and to hear the

tread of armed hosts marching to its destruction.
They are clowns who play to the rabble, or
selfish and designing men, who make use of
shibboleths, to discredit and ruin their compa-
triots and fellow citizens. When educated and
serious men, who strive to see things as they
are, as all cultivated minds must strive to get
real views of whatever they contemplate, utter
their honest opinions on this subject, a clamor
is raised against them, which would be of small
account, were it not for the fact that it tends to
make the calm and enlightened discussion of
this, our greatest national problem, difficult and
ineffectual. Our public thought crystallizes in
the mould of party and sect and clique and
faction, and they who refuse to narrow their
minds, but resolutely believe that it is possible
to live in the wide and tranquil realms of truth,
appear to be visionary and idle, or even perverse. Original and profound thinkers are rare
among us, because our ablest men are consumed
by politics and business, or driven into the noise
and confusion of endless controversy, or sacrificed to one or the other of our many schemes
for reforming the world and doing away with all
evil.

It is Emerson, I think, who said that he
would cross the ocean to talk with one great
man rather than to see all the monuments and

the treasures of art of Europe. Life is the subject of supreme interest. Everything depends
on power and quality of life. The school, however perfect the system, however admirable the
devices, can do the best work only when it is in
the hands of the best men and women. Education is, in a word, the stimulation of life, the
rousing of endowments to the activity which
produces faculty. As life proceeds from life, so
life is developed by life, and the kind of development depends chiefly upon the kind of life
by which it is promoted. The problem which
most deserves the serious meditation of the
lovers of human protection, who are also necessarily lovers of God and country, is how to
make the teacher's calling attractive to the men
and the women who possess in a high degree
power and quality of life, — so attractive as to be
followed as a life-work, and not taken up as an
expedient until something more pleasant, or
more secure, or more lucrative is offered. How
this may best be done is a subject which will be
found more and more worthy of deliberation in
these annual meetings of the National Educational Association. Its appellation is a good
omen, for it implies that our school system
should be a national system. A national system
would enable us to remove the schools from the
tainted air of politics, it would raise the standard

of the teacher's profession, it would make his position more secure, and the recognition of his work more certain. It is said that a people has the government which it deserves. Let us, coming down to a lower plane, content ourselves with affirming that a school board has the teachers whom it deserves. Would the directors cross, not the ocean, but the township or the county line in search of a real teacher? If it takes a hero to know a hero, it takes an educator, or at least an educated man or woman, to know an educator. Inferior teaching in the primary schools implies inferior education for the masses of the people, and for those even who enter the colleges and the universities. School barracks which contain five hundred or a thousand pupils, with class rooms into which sixty or eighty children are crowded, are not places of education, but places of repression, confusion, and perversion. In such environment neither the teachers nor the learners can do good work. There is no indifferent school; the school is good or bad, it improves or perverts.

Another matter which deserves attention is the number of school hours. Not length of time, but intensity of application, is the important thing in all spiritual effort, and to attempt to do mental work when one is mentally weary, is not merely useless, but hurtful. Study prospers only when the mind is vigorous and the heart fresh. Tired children exhaust the teacher, as a dull and heavy teacher wearies the class. The young are most sensitive to fatigue of mind, and if kept too long in the class-room, they become inattentive, indifferent, and careless, and a distaste for study and a dislike for the school and the teacher grows upon them. A real teacher will accomplish more in four hours than he could accomplish in six. His pupils will come to school with glad hearts, will apply themselves industriously, and will not leave the class-room like released prisoners. Plato found an argument for the belief that our souls have lived in other worlds, in the quickness and eagerness with which the boys of Athens learned. If we would labor effectively to develop a nobler race of men here in America, let us work for the teachers, let us strive to raise the standard of their professional life, to render their position more secure, their task more pleasant, their reward greater and more certain, that the teacher's calling may appeal not to the most active and intelligent young women alone, but to the most active and intelligent young men as well. Then, indeed, shall the boys and the girls of America learn with quickness and eagerness, and when they quit the school, they shall quit it as true lovers of intellectual and moral power, who are resolved to spend a lifetime in unfolding and upbuilding their own being and in helping their fellowmen.

THE END.